THE HEART OF A GANGSTA 3

Jerry Jackson

Lock Down Publications and Ca$h
Presents
The Heart of a Gangsta 3
A Novel by *Jerry Jackson*

The Heart of a Gangsta 3

Lock Down Publications
P.O. Box 870494
Mesquite, Tx 75187

Visit our website @
www.lockdownpublications.com

Copyright 2018 The Heart of a Gangsta 3

First Edition May 2018
Printed in the United States of America

This is a work of fiction. Names, characters, places, and incidents either are products of the author's imagination or are used fictitiously. Any similarity to actual events or locales or persons, living or dead, is entirely coincidental.

Lock Down Publications
Like our page on Facebook: Lock Down Publications @
www.facebook.com/lockdownpublications.ldp
Cover design and layout by: **Dynasty Cover Me**
Book interior design by: **Shawn Walker**
Edited by: **Sunny Giovanni**

Stay Connected with Us!

Text **LOCKDOWN** to 22828 to stay up-to-date with new releases, sneak peaks, contests and more…
Or **CLICK HERE** to sign up.
Thank you.

Like our page on Facebook:

Lock Down Publications: **Facebook**

Join Lock Down Publications/The New Era Reading Group

Visit our website @ www.lockdownpublications.com

Follow us on Instagram:

Lock Down Publications: Instagram

Email Us: We want to hear from you!

Submission Guideline

Submit the first three chapters of your completed manuscript to ldpsubmissions@gmail.com, subject line: Your book's title. The manuscript must be in a .doc file and sent as an attachment. Document should be in Times New Roman, double spaced and in size 12 font. Also, provide your synopsis and full contact information. If sending multiple submissions, they must each be in a separate email.

Have a story but no way to send it electronically? You can still submit to LDP/Ca$h Presents. Send in the first three chapters, written or typed, of your completed manuscript to:

LDP: Submissions Dept
Po Box 870494
Mesquite, Tx 75187

DO NOT send original manuscript. Must be a duplicate.

Provide your synopsis and a cover letter containing your full contact information.

Thanks for considering LDP and Ca$h Presents.

DEDICATION

I dedicate this book to ABG Mohawk and my nephew, Davion OGO Ringfield.

Y'all left us too early but heaven is where it's at, so congratulations, my little nephew and my slick partner, Mohawk.

Rest in peace.

ACKNOWLEDGEMENT

God first, y'all! I must take this given time to thank God for the grace He's blessed me with, the love, and most importantly, the protection through all my life's lessons. Without God, there is no *you* or *we*, so thank you, God, once again.

Cash, as always, thank you, brother. Thank you so much for being more than a business. Thank you for being even more than a friend, my brother. You have given me love and pushed me at all times, but never pushed me away. You have always welcomed me and motivated me to give me 100%. You bend over backwards, even when I'm speeding and moving recklessly. Thanks for showing me a brother's love.

Big Nard. Mr. East Hamp Champ— the first realest dude I've ever met, hands down with no cap. I love to brag about how we met, as well as how we are now. How it is? *Laughing out loud.* You're forever going to be the big homie of the city! Thank you, my nigga, for always telling me the right, solid shit, because playing the game fairly will get you a priceless blessing. You are, and forever will be my brother, my ace, my partner, and the realest nigga I know.

TJ, words can't do it, shawty. I got to try because I really never stressed these facts. I'm not going to sit and say you surprise me with how you have held me down for 17 years straight, non-stop. Anything I've ever asked you to do, fool, I swear you make it happen. It's always a yes, and when it's a no, I always hear it like I heard the yes you've said a million times. I love you, brother. I'm glad we're family, Brozay. I'm blessed to be your big brother, foo; real talk!

To my father— Sweet Z, Mr. Jackson— hey, man. Thank you giving me the most important details about life. You showed me, hands down, how to respect people with grace. You taught me great morals and invested in me some of the greatest sense. Our Life has been hard but our lessons has been priceless.

Ms. Anjelica Phelps, no lie, hands down, you are the most honest woman I've ever met in my lifetime. You are, without a doubt, the true love of my life. You are a Godly Black woman who strives even through the harshest moments. When you're weak, you display so much strength, and your faith is so amazing. I love you, ma'am. You're the one I respect like my ma, girl, and that's important. You're my best friend for life, my business partner, my ace, and my wife. Thank you.

Jessica Mann— my roll dawg, my support. Marijuana McCants, thank you forever. Can't wait to party. Aunt Pam; love you. All my cousins, my nieces and nephews, I love y'all. My brother, Chaney Jackson, love ya' fool. Twin, I love you still, but I'm still mad at you with lots of love. Nesha Baby, hold it down. I'm on the way. Cole Hart, I see you.

Free my brother, Swole. Love ya', foo, and everything you stand for. SilentMoney for life.

Jerry Jackson

Chapter 1
Icey

How could someone be so cruel, so evil and heartless to where they would stoop the lowest to bomb a funeral? Icey could not, for the love of God, wrap the answer of why around her mind. She looked at the TV in total disbelief of today's events. The news anchor was live on Northside Drive where the bombing took place. Icey could not believe someone actually killed the senator's daughter and her boyfriend in cold blood. Then, to make matters worse, their funeral had gotten bombed.

The news stated that it was 66 dead and another 38 seriously injured. It was shock and fear running through her. Fear because life was so dangerous in Atlanta, and shock because she had made a choice to come to Atlanta, Georgia with Pimp and this happened. Icey had truly thought she ran away from the drama, the killing the police, or anything bad-type of situations in Miami. She did not think it would be like this her first week here in Atlanta. No way possible.

The big question was if she made a mistake leaving Miami, following Pimp? Did she slip when leaving everything she'd work so hard to have in life? Why did she just drop everything the way she did? Was it the simple fact that she was pregnant with his seed? Did this fact hold any weight at all? Was love this powerful?

Icey found herself asking these questions and she still had not the slightest answer to either. All she had was hope. Hope and faith. She prayed that Pimp had pure intent in loving and wanting to be with her, and a great leadership capability because it was on him to carry them through whatever storm they should face. It would be up to him to see that they remained successful.

As she watched the news, her heart went out to the many victims that died and the families. Her heart was heavy with sorrow and pain because she could only imagine if it was her family member. On the TV screen, she noticed that some powerful and influential people were amongst those who were killed— police officers, lawyers and judges. Mostly the girl's entire family was killed because anyone seated up front was killed instantly. That was a pure shame, and the person who did this should be caught and punished.

A great shock came over Icey when she saw on the news channel her best friend Brad seated on the back of a fire truck. He wore over his face an oxygen mask. Standing around him were other federal agents in support of their respective friend. Even after seeing Brad okay, she was still fairly shaken, but now she was confused more than ever because all she could do was wonder. Why was Brad in ATL? Most importantly, what was he doing at these kids' funeral?

She reached for her phone and dialed his number with her heart beating rapidly in her chest. She wanted to give her support but his phone went to the voicemail after a few rings. Worried, Icey then called Pimp.

When Pimp's phone started ringing on her end, she also heard his ringtone right behind her, but at first she didn't catch it until the second ring. She quickly turned around to find Pimp looking at the news himself. Icey instantly got up and walked around the sofa to her man with a worried look on her face. She wrapped her arms around his neck and buried her face in his chest.

He wrapped his arms around her waist. "What's up, baby girl? How my baby treating you?" Pimp asked. His embrace was so warm and safe. She wanted it to last forever and ever.

"The baby is doing me fair but the news down here in Atlanta has scared me, baby. I'm not gonna lie. Like, have you seen this?" She pointed toward the TV.

Pimp looked at the TV for a second. He pulled his girl closer to him as a form of reassurance. "Baby, that could have happened anywhere. Plus, we don't stay near them anyways, baby. It's our actions against others when you're in constant contact with others that cause drama and problems. Me and you are not down here for friends. People don't know us, baby, and I plan to keep it that way." Pimp said this then kissed the side of her head.

"I hope you are right," she replied but wasn't convinced. She just wouldn't tell him of this doubt. She truly wanted to believe

Pimp, but at the same given token, she had her own common sense. Sense to go along with street smarts and book smarts. She would listen to him and pray her following wouldn't lead her to a disaster in this life's journey.

"I am right, baby. You is crazy if you thinking any other way," he arrogantly stated, then gave her another kiss. He let her go and went down to kiss her stomach. It was sticking out a little bit.

"I am not crazy, but I do believe what you say," Icey replied.

"I love you, woman," Pimp said and cut the TV off after he grabbed the remote control. He didn't want her to keep seeing the news. He wanted to get her mind off Brad's pussy ass anyways. *Fuck him*, Pimp thought.

"I love you, too." Icey started walking toward their bedroom while dialing a number on her phone. "I got to call Brad's mother." She was determined.

"For what?" Pimp followed.

"To let her know what's going on." She gave her man one of them *what do you think* looks.

Pimp didn't say anything else because he didn't want to make her think he was so concerned. Surprised himself, he didn't know Brad would be attending the funeral. If he had any knowledge of this fact, Pimp probably would've bombed the entire Church because it would be a joy to see him die.

"Okay, I'm 'bout to shower, baby girl. Come join me when you are done talking." He had to play it cool.

Him doing so worked in his favor when she looked up from the phone and replied, "I'm coming." Then, she went back to the phone call.

No matter if she and Brad weren't seeing eye to eye, she still couldn't help her love for their friendship. She wanted to see how his mother was doing and to let her know what had happened. Icey was just being the sweetheart she was known to be as the phone line began to ring.

Icey took a seat on the bed and was listening to the ringing of the phone. She was just thinking as it rung. She was looking down, but not at anything in particular, just lost in thought. She just was in a thoughtful stare when she noticed something strange. Icey fixed her eyes on the bottom of one of Pimp's shoes and noticed a yellow piece of a flower. At first, she just looked confused at it. Then, she bent down to get a closer look. She confirmed that it was indeed a flower. Icey hung up the phone pulled the flower from the bottom of Pimp's shoe and hid it so she could look at it later. She didn't want him to know she found it. Icey's head was spinning. She was hoping like hell that this wasn't what it appeared to be. She prayed Not.

Montay

Meco was standing in Montay's driveway, along with a few of his Shooters just standing around. Not only was Meco out at the house, so was Gangsta and Loco who were both posted in a G-wagon that was bullet proof, driven by a marksmen shooter.

Montay walked outside to greet his friends, his brothers, his team. These were the men who fed him and made him rich. He knew Gangsta wanted answers about this hit made on Rice Street, and the best way to discuss a serious matter was a face to face encounter. Montay knew it wasn't an issue that would cause a war between Pimp, nor the team, but it was still stuff that needed to be talked about. Montay knew basically what Gangsta was talking about. He was just hoping like hell Pimp saw the big picture and linked up with the cartel.

Pimp was one of those dudes who did their own thing. Montay knew this, and he was good at what he did and he answered to no-body. Montay knew Pimp could be a team player also because they just had handled good business down in Miami and in Atlanta, Georgia. He most definitely had to follow rules of the cartel because Gangsta had shit running smoothly. This could be the only problem for them. If Pimp wanted to just plant his feet in the city, he had to bow down to the bigger man.

Montay didn't even run or rule shit in the streets. Everything had to be approved and stamped by either Gangsta or Kash. Plus, it's hundreds of niggas under them that you had to go behind before you could come out popping in the city. Would Pimp see the big picture? Would he decide to leave and just respect the movement, or would Pimp be Pimp? These was the questions Montay asked in his mind. He was sure hoping like hell he saw the bigger picture.

Gangsta and Loco also got out the G-wagon. All the men greeted each other with dap and then Montay led them all to the other side of his house where they entered. Inside, it was a man's cave he only used for meetings and one on one talks amongst each other. It was exclusively laid. It was plushed-out with the best furniture money could buy.

Everyone found a comfortable place to sit as Montay started to fix drinks for those that indulge. Making their way over to the bar, Gangsta and Meco took seats at the stools.

Gangsta was well respected. He was considered a legend in Atlanta. He was the big homie to most and especially to Meco. Meco was a shot-caller himself. He was one of the dudes who held Atlanta down. He was the one who ran GF— the Atlanta gang— then everyone else, including Montay, fell in line.

"Grab me a soda, foo," Gangsta said.

"You know what I want, Don," Meco also added.

"Gotcha, and Pimp is in route," Montay said to Gangsta and Meco. He knew Gangsta wanted to hear that.

"Say less."

"He solo, right? It's enough new niggas as it is," Gangsta said while taking the Sprite given to him by Montay.

"Yeah, he by himself," replied Montay. Then, he fixed Meco his usual drink. He was hoping his statement was right because Pimp hadn't texted or called back yet. He gave Meco his drink then proceeded to make more shots for the Mob.

Loco soon joined the three at the small bar. He didn't drink like Pimp. Montay didn't really know Loco, but he knew he was with the cartel and he was like a brother to Kash and Gangsta. It was so many war stories about them that Montay always eagerly listened to all the time.

"How long the wait?" Loco asked. He didn't sit, he stood.

"Bruh said he in route," Gangsta informed his partner.

Loco nodded as his reply. He was fresh in silk attire. He was a real made man.

People knew the story on Loco and Gangsta and were amazed. His name alone carried weight, and people looked at him like he was some type of god. Niggas knew of the shootout with the Feds and heard the stories of Kash. They knew Loco had major pull, and those that went against the cartel did not survive at all, so the best bet was to link up with them.

Montay fixed the Mob their drinks before taking a seat with his own drink and joined the conversation. He needed a drink right now because his nervousness had him stranded with the unknown. Pimp held the key to his happiness right now because he was really trying to retire from the game and sit back and enjoy life. Pimp needed to get there and comply like he knew Pimp would. At least, that was what he wanted and prayed for.

Montay had been through hell and back with Pimp in Miami. Ain't no way he couldn't rock the way Montay needed him to rock when he had Pimp's back before.

It's like going with Gangsta's plan and rules, you would end up rich with them, and the streets would be in the palm of your hands. You would practically be a boss. Pimp had his own money and he was a major nigga already within itself, so it made the choice of choosing a team a hard one. It would only be right that they link up and get more money, but it took Pimp to have an open mind and see what could happen.

"So, Montay, tell Loco the shit you witnessed this nigga Pimp do," Meco said to his Mob brother.

Everyone was now sitting on sofas and chairs.

Montay stood there, first in thought. Then, he started telling a brief story of shit Pimp was capable of doing. "I firsthand saw this nigga take out two of the biggest niggas in Miami. He took over an entire project of niggas, and this lil' nigga ran an exclusive strip club in downtown Miami. Only thing stopped him was that the motherfucking Feds came down on him and he started beefing in the streets with niggas. The shit didn't mix. He a real solid nigga, though," Montay told Loco, who nodded as Montay explained.

Then, Loco spoke. "Yeah, my father and his father have rendered business a time or two. He has special training and is very wise; just a hot-head, though. 'Bout like Kash, if you ask me." Loco surprised everyone with the information he shared. Not even Gangsta knew Loco had intel on Pimp, but he did and he showed them that he really was plugged in everywhere.

Jerry Jackson

Chapter 2
Pimp

Pimp checked his phone and noticed that he had missed calls from Montay and a few text messages. He didn't call back or reply while leaving his house. Icey's mind had finally settled after he managed to calm her nerves. This made it easy for him to leave and catch this meeting, because if she was still tripping, then he would have to stand Montay up. He wanted and needed her comfortable.

Montay was lucky. Pimp wasn't into meeting new niggas anyway, but on the love and strength of Montay did he decided to pull up.

He was walking downstairs when he saw Icey going through a box in their massive living room. Pimp made his way over to his wife-to-be. He walked up behind her, catching her and turning her around to his kiss. "I'll be back. I wanna take you out after this meeting," he told her, still holding her close.

With another kiss, Icey smiled. "Okay, baby."

Every car Pimp purchased in Atlanta, he made sure to get bullet-proof and tinted. He chose to jump into his two-door Bentley Continental GT. He was fresh just like his car as he closed the door, embracing the Nappa leather. He pulled his gun out and placed it on the passenger seat. Young Thug came through the speakers when the Bentley came to life. He looked down at his phone again and tossed it also on the passenger's seat before pulling off.

Atlanta Georgia was the new start for him and Icey, and he would make the best of it for them both. He knew Icey thought he expected her to sit home and have kids, playing the wife role to its T. Icey had no idea that he had already started the process of building her art school as it was in Miami. He also wanted her to keep the original one up and running. *It was only right*, he thought. He just wanted her happy and not to feel trapped. He wanted to just get shit going perfectly for them as he awaited his father's return home. Today's traffic was thick and police patrol was extensive because of the bombing— something so deadly Pimp had caused— and yet his mind was on loving Icey and their unborn child.

Why was she so different from other females he met? What did Icey have on them? Sometimes Pimp even wondered if she put some kind of love spell on him. He was indeed in love and in like with her everything. She was this perfect female in his eyes. He just wondered why. Pimp reached for the radio to turn it down, simultaneously stopping at a red light.

The GPS said he was 45 minutes from his destination, and Pimp had realized he had not eaten anything. The feeling of hunger tested his stomach and toyed with his mind. He cut the music down to a soft sound and looked from side to side at all the restaurants. He needed to choose one before the light turned.

He quickly chose Sonic's and grabbed his ringing phone. It was Honey. He looked at it but didn't answer. He was too focused on this food. Pimp pulled up to the sign where the menu was posted after pulling into the parking lot. It only took a second for an employee to come out to take his order. Pimp ordered him a plate of chicken stripes and fries, then began to send Honey a text message.

As he texted, his phone started ringing again, but this time it was Montay. Pimp answered. "Yo."

"What's up? You on the way?" Montay asked.

"Yeah, 'bout a hour or less, I'll be there. Had to grab some food and shit," Pimp replied.

"Okay, cool. We here waiting on you, bro. I was just making sure you knew this was important. I have some important people here to talk to you," Montay said.

Pimp heard his voice but Montay wasn't sounding like himself. That's what made him pay attention. It sounded like Montay was nervous or something. Pimp just didn't say anything.

His food soon arrived, along with the slushy on the side. He instantly attacked his fries while putting the slushy inside the cup holder. Pimp pulled off from Sonic's and was back in traffic, digging in his bag. He stuffed his mouth with some fries, then used his pinky to cut the music back up.

Pimp shook his head in thought of how Montay seemed so pressed to get him there. He wondered what was so important. Pimp cared nothing about anyone being important. For all he cared, he killed important people as a way of life on a daily, so who was this dude or who was these niggas? He would soon find out.

Pimp had other plans, and right now, going along with others wasn't a good idea. Especially if Montay thought for one second Pimp was about to get back into the dope game or any of that stupid shit. Pimp was ready to do his own thing on another level, away from niggas and the street life. His only reason for being around Montay or any nigga for the matter was to use them to get to where he was going, and he had succeeded at doing just that. He saluted Montay for that but he wasn't the one trying to be used. He gave him loyalty and good friendship. Montay was cool and their fathers had history together back in the day, so Montay had the family part in tune.

It took Pimp under 45 minutes to finally make it to Montay's house. A house that had a bunch of big boy rides in its driveway. He pulled up in a spot, and even before he could cut the engine off, he saw someone come from the side of Montay's house. It was a Mexican dressed in all black with black shades and a gun on his hip. Pimp didn't panic. He remained calm.

Jerry Jackson

Chapter 3
Montay

When Montay got word that Pimp was outside, he was happy and ready to get this situation out the way. He was the first person headed to the entrance of the house to let Pimp in. Montay opened the side door, happy to see his partner. He stepped to the side to allow Pimp inside. "What's up, bro? Anything to drink?"

"I'm good, brother," Pimp replied.

Everyone else was seated as both guys walked over.

Montay introduced the squad first. "Pimp, this Gangsta, Loco, Kash and Meco—very important people." Montay looked at Pimp then turned to the group. "Fellows, this is Pimp, my true friend."

Gangsta stood up first and then pointed to the other members in the house that was not important, like security and Shooters before saying, "Let us have the room." He then waited.

Without replies, the Shooters and drivers followed Montay who led them to another room that had equal the entertainment.

Loco stood up and walked over to stand face to face with Pimp. Pimp looked back at the Mexican. Loco studied the young, baby face killa, seeing a resemblance of his father. Pimp had no idea who Loco was but he didn't speak, he just looked at him back. Montay walked back in by then.

Gangsta had everyone's attention. He made sure to look everyone in the face, making sure they were paying attention. "So, Pimp, we called you here for two reasons, brother," Gangsta said when he finally fixed his eyes on Pimp.

"So, what's up?" Pimp asked

"Word got to me that you made a move in my town. A classified move that took one of my men off count." Gangsta pointed to Meco. "He vouched for your character, your credit and other shit that go along with it, so without a doubt, that business got handled. But my lil' nigga has to live with that from being caught in the act of your movements," Gangsta finished.

"I'll handle his lawyers and his comfort while—" Pimp had begun to speak but he couldn't finish his statement.

Gangsta cut him right back off. "All that's handled already. Plus, it doesn't work like that down here. Just pay the ticket for that business and we good. But what I'm talking about is that you bringing the feds with you to our city with leaving Miami, and we got structure here in Atlanta that took hard work to establish, my nigga. Feel me?" Gangsta paused, then added, "Feds already on yo' tail here is what we saying also, my brother."

Pimp listened intently to Gangsta and then he spoke his peace on the matter. "I'm well aware of the procedure the FBI follow. They are just looking to see if I'm doing anything illegal because I was hot in Dade County. I'm moving right and I'm super clean. My plan is to just blend in to this situation. I'm not here to stir up nothing you guys got going on," Pimp explained.

Montay got up. "Bro, I was talking to Gangsta, and we think you should consider fucking with our movement." He jumped in with his two cents. He was really trying to get to the point.

Pimp wasn't into it though, and Montay saw it on Pimp's face because he knew more than any nigga there in the house what was going on with Pimp in real life.

"So, tell me this. What's your plans, my brother?" Gangsta wanted to know.

"Nothing major. Probably open up a restaurant. Really, my focus is my girl. She runs an art school and studio, so I'm having one built. Plus, I got a lil' one on the way, so I can't be doing too much. I'm done with these streets, though." Pimp gave his best answer.

Gangsta even nodded out of respect for Pimp's words.

"I feel that, my friend. So, how is your father?" Loco asked and got a strange look from Pimp.

He was clearly confused at the sudden response. Not too many people knew of his father, which only made it more confusing than anything.

Loco saw the look and smiled to give Pimp comfort. Then, he added, "Your father is friends with my family. Always been good business."

When Loco said this, it was then that Pimp understood loud and clear. He knew Loco was as serious as he appeared to be. Gangsta also bestowed that type of power. Pimp knew now how important the group was.

"Okay. Well, he's good. He's just getting old, that's all," Pimp replied.

"Yeah, I can help you out on the spots and areas on that restaurant business. You welcomed in our town, my nigga. Montay speaks so highly of you. We had to meet you though 'cause he said you was like Kash with the pressure," Gangsta told him.

Montay was happy with the whole meeting. So happy that he went to make more drinks. "We need to toast to this one."

"I'll pass," said Loco.

"I don't drink," Pimp added.

"Me either," Gangsta joined, and that was the first hand shake between him and Pimp.

Montay was the only one ready to drink, but feeling out of place he decided against it. He would come out better hanging with the shooters. However it went, he was extremely at peace now 'cause he could sit back and slip out the game. Montay just wanted to be the family man who had not even a pinky finger on the game. He just wanted to be done. He too held major hope that Pimp really fucked with Loco and Gangsta 'cause he was a perfect fit to what's going on with them. With Montay leaving the game, they would need a good replacement.

Pimp's mind was locked in on his own things. Things that didn't include the cartel. Pimp looked to Gangsta and said, "We most definitely need to link on that business though, bro." Pimp stood up so did everyone else.

"Facts," Gangsta replied.

All the men begun to leave after trading numbers and hand-shakes. They walked outside after getting the Shooters on point for their exit. The same two Mexicans that checked Pimp and let him in was out there waiting on the group. Everyone were in good vibes, especially Montay.

Pimp and Montay walked to his ride.

"Man, I'm glad you fucking with us. I knew you was gonna fuck wit cha boy anyways. Feel me?" Montay tossed one arm over Pimp's shoulder.

"I'm wit cha, my nigga. I know you got my best interest, bro," Pimp told him as they reached the Benz wagon. They gave each other dap before Pimp jumped in, cranking up. "I'll bust at you, bro."

"That's a bet, my nigga," Montay said, taking a step back.

Pimp put the car in reverse and pulled off. Gangsta and Loco also pulled off, leaving only the Mob there in the yard.

"Whoa! Wassup, foo?" Meco gave him one of their handshakes.

"Shit, foo. 'Bout to go spend this day with the family. You know I been gone a few months in Miami. Gotta get back good with the love ones," Montay informed his brother.

"I feel that, fooly. Well, we 'bout to pull out then, my nigga. Be safe and steady. Mob like a Don do," said Meco.

"Two love, foo."

"Twice." Meco jumped into his ride also with his brothers leaving a happy Montay standing there.

Montay's brothers, his friends, his team and even his wife didn't know that he had other plans, and it was over with for him. *They probably wouldn't even see him again, and that's real*, was his thought before walking back into the house.

Brad

Northside Drive was crowded with FBI and local cops trying to keep the streets calm and the many families that were out in despair. The entire street where the church was located was closed down due to the massive bombing, and the search for the suspects was massive. Local cops and some FBI agents had road blocks going either way on both ends of Northside Drive, stopping all vehicles that came and went.

Brad was still in the midst of things after medics checked and cleared him from the injured list. He quickly went right into action on the case because now it had become personal.

Atlanta wasn't his field office so he had to get approval to work, then he would sit back while agents from Georgia fields came through to aid him. This did not stop him from beginning to do ground work on building the case as he waited to be cleared. It took the evidence response team at least 8 hours to process the crime scene good enough so that bombing experts could get in there to see exactly where the bombs were placed.

Bodies were still being pulled from the pile of a three-story stone and brick church that had nearly crumble down. Brad, along with many more agents, waited impatiently for the crime scene to open up so they could get in there too and work. It was very personal to many agents, so finding any evidence, any leads, any clues would be great for them all.

It was very, very personal to Brad 'cause he lost a good friend over a ruthless, heartless reason. All he could think about was this case right now. He had to find the person behind this act for the sake of Jimmy. He couldn't just let him die in vain.

Brad and another agent was in conversation when they noticed that four black on black Sprinters pulled up. It had to be very important people because, when nobody could get under the tape, the vans were allowed onto the classified grounds. This only meant these folks were very important. As doors were opened, Brad watched as the FBI detective agency climbed out, approaching the crime scene. Then, Brad was taken aback by Beauty.

When she stepped out the van, in conversation on her phone with only a pad in her other arm, pressed against her small waist, you could easily tell she was the boss— the one in charge. Brad and every other man around who had love for Beauty could not help but notice this woman was bad. Even from a distance you could see her sexy face and amazing figure. She was a black woman at that, which made it look even better.

Brad had to remain professional at all times, so he quickly turned his attention elsewhere with his memory full of this woman.

The estimated time of him getting to the scene was at least 8 more hours and darkness had already taken the sky. Brad decided to go get a shower and change of clothes. It was not until he got into his car that he noticed the many, many missed calls from his mother and Icey.

These actions alone made Brad smile 'cause he needed to feel that love. An amazing feeling of love, especially from Icey— his sister, his best friend.

Chapter 4
Trish

Trish Williams was the supervisory commander at the crime scene. Even with her youthful look radiating you could still see that she had pure leadership how she got right on top of things. Pulling the phone from her ear she called one of her agents over. "Have every neighborhood coordinated through every county from east to west." Trish looked from a distance at the bombed church. It was some bad damage she noticed as she began to walk with her agents. "Also, get me the first official on the scene, a list of every witness, and, or survivor."

"Will do, boss," the young agent said and walked off to do as he was told.

The church was 65% destroyed, Trish noted as she got closer. The scene was quite chaotic and had nearly a hundred agents on the job. Trish pulled out her ID card and introduce herself. "Supervisor and commander in charge. Where is the senior?" She spoke loud enough so those around her to hear. She instantly got the respect being the boss had brought.

"I'm special agent Gordon, responsible for processing the scene. Our commander is at post but I can certainly update you on what we have thus far," the older man said to her. He was Black as well and Trish liked that. It was good seeing her kind in success in life.

"Great. I'm all ears." Trish spoke but not diverting her eyes from looking over everything.

"Okay, so far we have two explosions, both hidden in the caskets. No suspects, and eighty-one dead. Nearly all the immediate family was killed in the blast. Bodies are still being pulled out as we are speaking," the agent told Trish while actually looking at another body hidden by a body bag that was being led to the ambulance. "Also, we have a multi-agent task force joined, knowing it will take a few days to assemble all the evidence," he said.

She took everything in while still looking around. "Has any team been sent to the funeral home?" Trish asked and found a confused look on the agent's face. This only meant that someone hadn't been doing their job.

"I'm not certain—"

"Good evening, ma'am. Gregory Jones, senior detective," another man approached and interrupted them with respect. He and Trish shook hands.

"Commander Williams, sir. Tell me what you have so far," said Trish. She needed to get straight to the point. It was no time to waste because the more wasted time, the further the perpetrator got away and the harder the case becomes.

The detective began explaining in greater detail the real extent of the investigation. Trish listened though still looking around as they walked.

She listened, and even with her extreme professionalism, her mind still escaped her work and found its notion on her lovely husband. She was just missing him and hated the fact that she had to leave his embrace this morning.

The detective stopped at the entrance of the church so that another body bag could be haul out. This was the only thing that stopped Trish mind from being lost on her husband. She looked on and continued listening to the detective. After the body bag passed them, they stepped inside the crumbled church, not knowing what they would see or learn.

Trish followed the detective and suddenly stopped in her tracks when she noticed multiple dead people just laying all over the place. Chills rushed over her body. Her heart got heavy. She knew this was going take some time. She pulled out her phone to send Veedoo a text telling him to not expect her home. As bad as she wanted to go home, Trish knew it was about to be a long night.

Icey

Icey wanted badly to trust Pimp but it was too many signs of him doing these devious things that keep popping up right in her face, no matter if she was looking or not. She tried desperately to ignore the obvious but it was hard doing so with this evidence found, and even with being in love she still had to have common sense enough to know if things were not correct. She did have intuition and a gut feeling. Pimp must not forget that.

She was literally having second thoughts about everything with Pimp. She wondered if she'd ask Pimp about the flower, would he tell her the truth? But did she even want to know the truth? Could she handle the truth? She didn't know, but she did want Pimp to just sit down. She just wanted to be happy and safe. She wanted to be a family and in love. Didn't he know she was pregnant? He sure didn't act like he knew.

Icey noticed her phone begin to ring and saw that it was Brad. Her heart smiled as she quickly pressed accept to take the call. "Hello!"

"Icey, how you doing?"

"Brad!" She couldn't help but to show every bit of the pure concern she had for her friend. She was glad to hear his voice. She missed her friend. "Question is how are you?" asked Icey. She was happy but very concerned for him.

"I'm blessed, I know that much. But Jimmy didn't make it," Brad told her with cracks in his voice.

The news shocked and hurt Icey because Jimmy was a good dude. He had a big heart. He had a wife and kids.

Icey was crushed. "Lord, Brad, I'm so sorry to hear that. Oh my God, what happened? Jesus Christ, Brad, are you serious?" She started crying.

"It's okay, baby girl. We're going to find the person who did this and make them pay for it. I promise you. I need you to be strong, too, okay?"

It took a brief moment of her crying before she straightened up and calmed down enough to talk. "You right, you right. But, Lord, that's a shame," Icey said heart broken.

"I know. So, how are you in your new life?" Brad asked.

"Atlanta is no different than Miami, I have found out. My question to you is, what brings you here? I'm still trying to put together how you ended up at this church is what I'm saying."

Badly he wanted to lie to Icey. To rock her to sleep with a lie, but at the same time he wanted to mend their friendship. Brad was missing his best friend, and if they were to start back talking again he wanted everything to be extremely honest. He knew she would not understand, but still she needed to know the truth. Or did she? Could he actually tell her that he was really down in Atlanta to save her and to arrest her man? She would go crazy; no questions about it. With all this said and done after careful thought, Brad decided to fix himself to tell her a lie. He knew Icey would never understand.

"We had to do an escort from state to state with the mayor from Miami. When me and Jimmy took the detail, we didn't know we'd end up at the church. Hate that we didn't stay in Miami. Jimmy would be here with us." He wanted to get off that subject though. It was getting to him again.

"Oh, well, it would be good to see you before you leave and head home. Maybe we can hang out. So, when do you leave?" Icey wanted to know.

Brad was kind of struck at the question. "I'm not sure but I think we can make something happen. All I gotta see is the date and I'll let you know," he told her, but really didn't know if it was a good idea or not.

"Sounds good to me. So have you spoken with your mother yet?"

"Actually, I haven't but need to, so let me ring her and I'll call you afterwards." Brad jumped right into it. Neither one of them were big on making their mother worry about them.

"Okay, I love you," Icey said.

"I love you too, baby girl. You be careful," Brad spoke and quickly ended their call.

Just speaking to Brad made her feel better. It made her feel loved, it made her miss Pimp and it made her want to see him. She sent him a quick text asking what time he'd be home. It was getting late. She had the piece of flower on their nightstand because her plan was to confront him about it, but now she decided against it. She really didn't even want to know the answer.

After sending the text, she started unpacking the smaller stuff, leaving the larger, heavier things to Pimp when he finally did sit down and breathe.

Icey was unpacking a box that contained some of her important paperwork from her school and business. She began to read over most of her accomplishments. She missed her school and most of all her students. Was she just too emotional? Had the pregnancy overrode her emotions that much? She was really giving up her Miami life for an unknown one with Pimp, all because she was pregnant. Icey worked so hard to get to where she was, and just to give it all up for the sake of love had her more confused than ever.

She had to put all the stuff back in the box and grabbed more clothes to put up before she started crying again. As she got up to walk to her walk-in closet, she thought about how she didn't have any friends in Atlanta. She was alone and out on the faith of love. What if it didn't work? Would she be able to pick up where she left off back home? Yeah, she just needed to sit down, gather some thoughts and most importantly rest her nerves.

She left the closet and walked out of their master bedroom. Icey found herself downstairs in the kitchen, seated at the table. She tried to find a piece of mind at that moment 'cause life was moving fast right now. The phone started ringing which scared her just a bit. She quickly picked up though her heart was beating.

"Hello?" Icey answered.

Jerry Jackson

Chapter 5
Trish

Trish was back at her desk at the command post in downtown Atlanta. She had piles of notes and paperwork in front of her— important papers she had to go through. The scene on Northside Drive was still being processed. She was more frustrated with the fact that still she had yet to get statements from the funeral director.

She shook her head while standing from the desk. Why couldn't she just be home, relaxing with her husband? Outside her office she made a cup of coffee when two agents walked up.

"Mrs. Williams, the meeting room is available."

"Okay, give me two minutes, tops," said Trish. She had totally forgotten briefing, due to her mind being someplace else. She needed to establish herself with this new team of field agents that were from Miami, plus the detectives and the forensics psychology team. Trish grabbed all the important papers and stuffed them into a folder. She got her coffee and headed to the briefing room.

Trish entered the room of at least 30 field agents and head officials. Bomb experts and explosive device experts also were amongst those. The attorney general was also there, already in discussion when she walked in, so Trish found her spot and watched the film of evidence.

Veedoo texted her phone saying that he loved her and couldn't wait to see her again. He said this as if she wasn't just with him a few hours ago. The gesture made her smile and get lost in thought about her wonderful husband. Trish was so glad that they had met and that she had given him the chance he deserved. Veedoo was an amazing husband and a very successful man at that. He was completely out of the streets, thank God. All he did was take care his kids and Trish. It seemed like her husband was this perfect fit to her life, and every day she thanked God for their marriage. It was hard at first for them but with prayers and support and true love from each other, they made it work.

Being in the FBI made things even more bad because Veedoo had been prosecuted on federal charges before, and it was a time when he attempted to retire from the game. Trish had to make a grave decision to either help Veedoo and marry him, or arrest him and break her own heart. Her career was also on the line. She could end up in jail herself if she helped him, and that's the chance she took.

She wanted the relationship her and Veedoo had started and came to love. She wanted it to work badly. So bad that she could merely taste it. Veedoo was 100% man and she adored every bit of him as much as he did her.

Veedoo also proved to be true to his words and never went back to the dope game or did anything illegal when she cleared him and his whole team. That was the only time ever had she violated her job, and she told Veedoo that she would never do that again, and Veedoo had to respect her. However, he did still remain friends with his street friends. All of them also respected Veedoo's wish to get out the game and even encouraged him at times that it was a good thing. Eventually, he saw that it was.

***

The next day, Trish was armed with a search warrant, a forensic team and four agents. They headed down to the funeral home's chapel where the bodies of the dead were prepared. Trish also had a team go to the funeral director's home with a search warrant which was only two blocks up.

Luckily the funeral home was still open and Trish had men go serve him the warrant. Outside, she waited at the door, seeing the lab tech enter, and then two agents escorted the director up to the front office. The office was quickly swept for bombs and then Trish was ushered in. Moments later, the old man seemed confused.

"Special agent Williams, FBI," Trish introduce herself at the same time she handed over to the director some paperwork. "I'm here to ask you a few questions. Also, we have a search warrant."

The director looked over the paper and carefully read from it before looking back up to the agents. "Okay. Be my guest."

"I need to see all records of recent services provided by you. Do you have surveillance?"

"I don't have surveillance but I can grab the paperwork you requested."

"Could you tell me of anything strange around here?" Trish asked.

"Not to my knowledge," the director stated and started going through paperwork, looking for files to hand over.

Trish was surveying the office— the point of entry and any other possible way to get past the director unnoticed. "Has anyone other than the family inquired about the bodies? Has anyone strange entered your establishment?" Trish asked.

The director was going through files but still managed to answer over his shoulder. "No. No one strange or no other people other than the father and mother of the deceased has come here." He turned with papers in his hands and gave them to Trish.

"What about any other business?"

"Well, yes. As you can see, I have great business here."

"Okay. I'd like those files, too," Trish added. "Try to remember anything."

The director was being as cooperative as possible. Trish had a team of agents going up and down the streets looking for any witnesses. She joined the forensic team downstairs as they dusted and swept for any evidence.

She was looking hard around, trying to process what had happened, then her phone rang on her hip. "Agent Williams."

"The bombs that were planted inside the caskets? Lab results just came back in. They were remote controlled. Some one knew what they were doing," One of the bomb experts called and confirmed.

"Okay. Good to know, because I'm here at the funeral home."

"Great. It starts there."

Trish knew then that the case would take another turn. Was it the funeral director who was involved? She surely hoped not. Trish made her way back upstairs to question the director again because something wasn't right with this picture.

Jerry Jackson

Chapter 6
Brad

The very next morning Brad and a team of agents were assigned the task of going corner to corner, to store to store looking for any witness that could offer them up a good lead.

Walking down the opposite side of the funeral home, the morning air felt good. Brad decided to speak with the drug users and drunks of everyday living, even though it was a longshot, and usually drunks and drug addicts were not a good source to gather intel from. Brad was kind of desperate and needed something, anything to go on.

As he was walking he saw this couple sitting in a cut, surrounded by old boxes and other things that made it seems as if an attempt was made to build a shelter. Brad knew from the looks of things that the couple was accustomed to this spot but they actually lived there.

He walked over, revealing his ID, introducing himself. "FBI. I need to ask the two of you a few questions."

Instantly the couple got defensive. The dude who was heavy in weight scrambled to his feet as his girl was secretly grabbing all their illegal contraband. Brad saw her but he was not thinking about arresting them for something so petty. He did take caution, stepping backward as he was watching the Man.

"Man, we haven't done anything!" the big guy stated, trying to be as intimidating as he possibly could be but the gesture didn't work on Brad.

"You are not in trouble. Calm down." Ready to reach for his gun, Brad took another cautios step back with his hand held out to keep the guy at bay.

"What's wrong then? Why you messing with us?" They wanted to know.

"Like I said, I'm here to ask a couple questions. Did you hear about the bombing that happened?" Brad began.

"Nawl—"

"Northside Drive, you mean?" the woman cut in.

"Exactly," Brad confirmed.

"Nawl, we don't know nothing about no bombing." Big guy looked at his girlfriend with one of those looks and she instantly got the picture, but Brad wasn't having it.

"Sir, I'm now speaking to the lady—"

"My woman! And like I said, officer, we haven't heard anything at all." The dude was playing hard ball and Brad wondered why. As bad as he wanted to pressure them, he didn't. He just calmly walked off.

He continued to survey the area near them and then casually walked off down the alley full of other people. He could faintly hear the couple get into a heated argument, probably because the woman knew something and nearly spilled the information to Brad. Brad asked a few more people the same questions as the first couple and nobody saw anything. Most had nothing to say at all and those that did talk only tried to sell the information. That was against all policy to purchase information from people and Brad had to remain professional, so he left. When he got back to the front of the alley, the couple was no longer there. Upon further inspection, Brad saw the woman standing outside a liquor store looking as if she was waiting on her man.

Brad knew it was now or never to speak with her or slip her one of his cards. He started in her direction, deciding he would pass her a card and hope like hell she'd call with some information. As Brad approached her, he held out his card visibly. She noticed him and froze, first looking into the store where her man was. She saw that he was still in line. Brad walked by and slipped her his card.

When she took it and cuffed it did he have confidence that she was on his side and that she really wanted to help him. Brad kept going, feeling good about being here to help. He joined the rest of the team and everyone brought to the table what they had found, heard or learned.

Inside the office again, Brad got blessed with the sight of the beautiful commander as everyone was taking seats, about to compare notes and statements. He couldn't help but be captivated by her youthful appearance and in charge demeanor. Before he could even ask himself the question of her relationship status, he noticed a sizable ring on her finger and his hope was crushed.

Trish was preparing papers at a desk as Brad looked on in lust of the woman. He wondered if her husband in law enforcement also, or if he was some big-time lawyer or something. He was a lucky man was all Brad could say.

Jerry Jackson

Chapter 7
Honey

Honey had a nice town house in Covington, Georgia right outside DeKalb County. Pimp chose this place because of the nice remote area. It didn't hold much traffic so Pimp crept over there early that morning. He was low-key. Pimp plan to keep it that way too.

Honey was in the shower while Pimp got dressed from a good morning fuck— something she ain't had in a while. He picked up his phone and saw that Icey had sent him a message that she woke up. He didn't reply. Instead, he prepared to leave, being that he had more business to tend to and he had to get back home.

He grabbed his gun and put it on his hip. In his pockets were his phone and his car keys. It was a couple hundred thousand dollars spread across the bed. He left it there for her to put up in the new safe.

Pimp walked into the large bathroom where Honey was in a shower full off mist. "Baby, I'm out of here. Handle that money and hit me tomorrow when you send that money to your daughter," he said while looking at her figure through the glass.

Honey peeked her head from around the glass. Her long hair was wet and hanging. She was looking beautiful. "Okay, baby. That's what's up. Lock that door downstairs," Honey said.

Pimp had made arrangements for her daughter to come stay with her. She just didn't know. He knew she would like this fact and it helped with him not being around so much. Her daughter would occupy half the time he would. He needed Honey in Atlanta with him but he wasn't trying to go into any relationship or nothing near it with her. He had business in mind for her instead of using her and leaving her. This time he had plans for her to be around.

Pimp jumped into his G wagon and sent Icey a text, telling her he was on the way home. He stayed an hour outside of Honey's house which was a good thing because he didn't need her or Icey to bump heads for any reason at all. He crank up by push-to-start and got comfortable as he reversed out of the driveway.

Today had been a productive morning for him thus far and all of what he had going on. He felt like the chance for his father's freedom was so close and in their favor. He couldn't wait until that day when his father was released. But for right now, he would establish himself and his small family in this big city. He would go into this shell somewhat, calm down and raise his child and build his business.

Pimp had always been the smart and driven type of person in life anyway. He was the young guy who liked school and learning new things. He also knew how to play the streets. He knew how to be the most vicious killer to the slickest drug dealer or to the hardest niggas. Atlanta, Georgia was a fresh start and he was about to make it be a lasting one.

As Pimp drove the highway his phone started ringing from an unknown number, meaning it was his father calling. He turned the music down that was playing and answered. "Pops, what's going on?"

"Yo, how are you, son?" his father asked. It was a code letting Pimp know he was worried. It had to be that he'd seen the news of the bombing.

"Everything is good, especially me. What's going on with you though? I had spoken with the lawyer. She got things moving along." Pimp decided to hit him with some good news and hope it put him at ease. Every man and woman in prison deserved that feeling of love when being locked up.

"Yeah, she just came to visit me yesterday. When are you showing up?"

"This weekend," Pimp replied. He needed to holla at his father anyway because he had some questions about Loco and these niggas in Atlanta. He knew his father was still plugged in with the know and he was one person Pimp trusted whole-heartedly.

"Okay, son, that sounds like a plan," was his father's reply.

"Okay, I'll see and talk to you then, pops."

"How is that girl you got pregnant? When is she due?" Pops asked.

"Oh, everything good, pops. She got 'bout five more months."

"Okay, son. Well, we will finish this conversation on the weekend. You be careful out there and I'll be safe in here."

"That's fair. I'll see ya' soon, pops."

They ended the phone call. Pimp put the phone on the passenger's seat and focused on the road ahead of him. He was ready to get home and around his wife-to-be. He was ready to lay in his bed for once. It took him the full hour to get home but when he pulled up in his driveway, he was so happy to be home, safe and out the streets that he just sat there in the G wagon lost in thought, in a comfort mode.

He was so in thought that he didn't see Icey walk outside and around to the passenger seat. When she tapped on the window it made him jump from being crept up on. Pimp caught his composure and unlocked the door for her. At the same time, he was moving his gun and phone. He wasn't fast enough though because Icey still saw the gun and hesitantly climbed into the G wagon and closed the door.

"Hey." Softly she spoke.

"What's up, baby girl?" Pimp leaned over and kissed her before settling back into the seat.

"Nothing. I was in the kitchen when you pulled up, and when you didn't come inside I watched you sit here in a daze. I gave you five minutes but I had decided to join. So, what's up? What's on your mind?" Icey asked. She looked at the man that had her pregnant. The man she was in love with and was willing to spend the rest of her life with. She just wanted to know and wanted to hear that everything was going to be alright.

"Oh, everything with me good, baby. I was just thinking about the surprise I have for you, whether I should tell you now or just wait. That's why I didn't come right inside, baby. I'm straight, though, baby. Just miss you, that's all." Pimp had to tell her to put her at ease.

"Okay, baby. I love you. Let's go in," Icey stated, and they shared a kiss before the both of them got out the ride.

Pimp followed his sexy baby's mother into their home. Icey went back into the kitchen where she had fixed her a bowl of fruit.

She sat at the table and Pimp joined her, reaching into the bowl then stuffing his mouth. She was on Facebook so she picked her phone back up. Briefly Pimp checked his phone for any message and saw none.

"Baby, you said that you had a surprise for me. So, what was it?" Icey asked but didn't take her eyes away from the screen.

Pimp smiled and got up, going into the refrigerator. He spoke over his shoulder. "I said that I didn't decide whether I would tell you or not, so don't put no words in my mouth."

Icey, smiling, also stood to her feet. She had her hand filled with fruit. She came close to him. "Why can't I know? You should've never said anything about it. Now I wanna know," said Icey, eating fruit.

"I'll give you a hint," Pimp teased.

"Okay."

"It's gonna be like Miami, Forida."

"Huh?" That statement alone confused her.

Pimp smiled but this time he walked upstairs to their bedroom. Icey stayed in the kitchen to finish her fruit.

Pimp took in the view of their large bedroom that was not fully ready. He walked into the room more, knowing tomorrow he would have to hang around and help her unpack. He took a seat on the softness of the mattress and began to remove his shoes.

Pimp's heart nearly stopped when he noticed something. Not in a million years did he think he would see one of or a piece of the flower from the funeral home on his nightstand by the bed he shared with Icey. How did it get there was the first question. Did he slip like that? Did he even put the shit there? Pimp knew he didn't put the flower there. Hell, he couldn't even remember obtaining the flower. A ripped piece at that.

He reached out and took it in his hand. He knew it was from the funeral home but how did it get here? As Pimp retraced his steps he put in his mind that it had to stick to his clothes and fall off in the house, but why was it on the nightstand was the next big question that needed an answer. The first person that came to mind was his girl Icey.

Veedoo

Since Trish wouldn't be home in time for dinner, Veedoo decided to come out tonight for one of his partners' birthday parties. Veedoo was far out in the streets and everyone knew and respected it. He had better vision and started his own cleaning service, a youthful gym and training school. Veedoo also was the owner of a lucrative trucking company in New Jersey.

Really, all he did was watch the money grow. He sat back and raised his two kids who were teens now and needed his direct attention. His team was still doing their thing. He would always have their backs and they knew it.

He got fresh in a designer shirt and denim jeans with a few pieces of jewelry to show his status was still at boss level. Atlanta knew Veedoo and his squad. For those who didn't, best believe somebody will tell them.

Tonight, niggas and bitches were going to know what was up with him when he pulled up, driving a sports Bentley Continental GT with a dope boy color and high-priced rims. Tonight, he was strapped because it was protocol that he be, even with his team being the face of the party. Security was going to be tight. He would still be on alert for the haters, because no matter what, when you are up and doing you, niggas go to hating and Veedoo knew this.

Some people would call his life lucky. Some would say that he was blessed but Veedoo called it hard work that paid off. See, what people failed to realize was that nobody did 10 years for him but him, and it wasn't easy at all. And the struggle was real when he finally hit the streets and saw how shit was going firsthand. It took a lot of effort and loyalty for him to get his money right.

Nobody but Gangsta gave him the chance and Veedoo didn't look back from it, but as soon as he got right in the pocket, he wanted to get right in life. That's when he met his wife and life really changed for him.

The party was held in the Velvet Room. It took Veedoo not long to get there due to him living in the area. When he pulled up, the parking lot was crowded with big money and heavy security. As Veedoo maneuvered the Bentley to a place to park he noticed Loco and his family entering the building. Then he saw Kash and Meco lingering in the commotion of people just talking to each other.

Today was Monkey's birthday. He was like a brother to Gangsta. He had been around a few years and proved to be solid as Gangsta said he was.

Veedoo jumped out the Bentley and got with Kash and Meco. Everyone dapped each other.

"What's up, foo?" Meco spoke.

"Man, I'm just here, foo," Veedoo shot back.

"Let's go 'head and slide in. Gangsta and Monkey already inside that bitch," Kash stated and the entire squad followed his lead.

When they made it inside the club it was easy to see who the birthday boy was. Monkey was iced out and talking shit with a drink in his hand and money in the other. Veedoo also saw Gangsta in the area. Monkey was every bit of solid people thought he was. Him and Gangsta were like brothers because of his loyalty and his grind mode. This fact had earned him a major spot, and now Monkey was considered a factor in Atlanta, Georgia and two other states. He was still heavy in the drug trade, operating under a cartel led by Kash and Gangsta. Even with his drug business he still had a very lucrative construction company in Minnesota and was part owner of two five-star restaurants in Atlanta. Veedoo made his way over to his partner and to wish Monkey a happy birthday.

Gangsta had saved his life twice. He would always give him loyalty and he was family in Veedoo's eyes. Hell, Gangsta was the reason for everyone's come up, and for that he was thankful.

"What's up, playboy? Happy G Day." Veedoo eased into the crowd. He showed love to Monkey then found Gangsta. "Sup, fooly?"

They gave each other dap.

"What's happening? You looking good, my brother," Gangsta replied humbly as he stood.

"I'm feeling good, bro. Business is A-1, life is beautiful and my team is safe," Veedoo told him.

Gangsta understood and nodded his reply.

Veedoo knew all Gangsta cared about was his operation going smoothly. All he ever asked Veedoo to do was to make sure his wife Trisha didn't come after them with federal charges. Veedoo also had to seal the deal with a promise that no one would pop up on the federal radar because everyone knew that Trish would do her job. Veedoo also knew that Gangsta knew he would murder his wife on-call if need be because not even love was more important than the operation.

"How the kids?"

"You already know, man. They getting bigger by the day, and spoiled rotten," said Veedoo to the question asked by Gangsta.

Veedoo also saw Gangsta's wife amongst those and Ne-Ne hardly ever came outside. It was more females there too. Veedoo knew most of them if not all as the music pumped.

The music stopped and the DJ jumped on the mic. "Yo! It's some real millionaires in this place tonight and a birthday player who run our city! Y'all pull up and put on for my nigga, the birthday guy!"

The music crank back up and the club went wild again as everyone started showing Monkey love with hugs and handshakes.

Veedoo found him a place to sit. It was right by Loco, one of his sisters and some bodyguards. Drinks and smoke was being passed around and each one Veedoo turned down because he was there just to show his support.

"What's going on, brother?" Loco shook his hand.

Gangsta joined them.

"What's good, Loco? How is Chavez?" Veedoo asked.

"He's making it, daily," Loco replied and slid over so either him or Gangsta could sit.

The club was packed and the party was going good.

"That's good. Everything else is lovely though," Veedoo said, and when he did, him and Loco locked eyes with each other with a certain amount of understanding. Basically, Veedoo told him that it's nothing to worry about and business could continue to run.

Gangsta trusted Veedoo to the core so he gave him the power to not touch noting illegal, and he could shut down every illegal operation the cartel had going if he made that call and everything would stop suddenly. As long as Veedoo told them things were good, then things were good.

Kash soon joined them at one of the VIP tables. He had a full bottle in his fist, he was fresh as he'd always been, he was crunk tonight and messing with all the pretty girls. Everything was lovely. Everyone was loving tonight and this was just what Veedoo needed.

Life was beautiful but behind the good was so much bad. Him and his squad had come a long way and by God's grace he's still eating with his same click he struggled with. Loco and Kash fell into a conversation and Veedoo's mind fell off to just being happy at the moment.

Chapter 8
Trish

Trish wanted all agents, one by one, in her office to hear what they heard or saw. Especially the ones who were at the crime scene when it happened. It was nearly 2AM and she wasn't close to being finished interviewing the agents. She only had four interviews already without anything important coming up. One thing she knew as an FBI agent was to never give up and always look at the unthinkable.

Her next interview was with an agent who was actually at the church before the bombing happened. Trish was glad to let him inside while introducing herself. "Special agent Williams."

"Special agent Brad, ma'am," he replied. He was a white man, tall and muscular with brown hair. He had some rough sights about him, but as big as he was he wasn't so intimidating.

"Have a seat, sir. So, I read that you were there before anything happened. Am I right?" asked Trish.

Brad took his seat with a nod of his head. "Yes, unfortunately I was."

"Okay. What I need to know is everything you did that lead up to this moment. Can you recant the same thing as is?" Trish wanted a clear picture of the things that went down.

It took Brad all but ten minutes to explain the process of his day. "And once me and my partner got to the church, we stood at the back. Things had happened fast after that because as I know, next was Jimmy helping an elderly woman get seated up front with her family, and then the explosions. After that, I couldn't really see anything else."

Trish took in everything the agent was saying. "Did you see anything strange, or anyone out of place? Had you heard anyone saying anything?" asked Trish.

"Nothing at all."

"What about any witness? Have you helped canvas the area?"

"Ma'am, yes, I spoke to a few people but none had anything worthy," Brad told her. He didn't mention the couple and the feeling of thinking they knew anything. He wanted to keep that in the cut just in case the woman did decide to call.

Trish asked him a few more questions and then she allowed him to leave. She was tired herself and wanted nothing more but to rest under her wonderful husband right now. She couldn't wait to get home.

Chapter 9
Monkey

The party was still lit as females danced and men gawked with keen interest. The music was so loud that you could literally feel it vibrate through your body. The temperature was up because of the drinks, smoke and massive body heat.

Sweat poured down Monkey's face and neck as he bounced around to the music with four or five females dancing with him. Monkey nor none of his friends or family noticed the danger that lurked in the cut of the club— a group of niggas hating the entire night.

The hate was real anywhere and it could be with anybody at any time, so you had to be prepared.

Gangsta was making his exit with Ne-Ne and Loco, taking with them half the security team.

Veedoo was getting ready to leave also when he walked over and gave Monkey a hug, and that's when shit just didn't feel right. Veedoo scanned the area and noticed the out-of-place niggas sitting in the cut. This was a private event though so them niggas Veedoo peeped had to be either friends or family, shit just didn't look right. It was easy to point them out because they were older than the crowd of people.

Veedoo was a street nigga and it just did not feel right, so he decided to say something to warn Monkey. "Yo, you be safe and watch them niggas that's over by the DJ booth. They on yo' game hard."

Nodding, he understood and showed the same love. "Sayless."

After Veedoo walked out, two more friends walked up on Monkey and he totally had forgotten about what Veedoo had just told him.

"Bro, we 'bout to push. You straight, right?" asked one of his friends.

"Yeah, I'm good, bro." Monkey dapped both friends and eased on through VIP where Kash was talking with a fine ass female.

Monkey walked up behind him and threw his arm over his shoulder, taking his attention.

"That birthday boy! Wassup, fooly? You good?" Kash asked.

"Hell yeah. I'm finna end my night, baby, and take me two bad bitches to go. I was just hollin' at you before I dip."

"Bet that. You ain't doing nothing wrong," Kash reminded him

Monkey had come to the club with security and that was how he planned to leave. He was three-deep but with the two strippers he planned on taking, it would be five. He was tipsy and more than high on two different drugs. As he moved toward the door, so did the group of men who were laying in the cut.

Monkey and his security made their exit followed by the two strippers. Outside, the parking lot was somewhat crowded with people going and coming. Most folks posted up at the first gas station available, this was the time you either getting something to snack on or some Gas.

VIP had his whip ready when they made it to the parking area. Monkey climbed inside the whip then came the strippers. It was his night, and never in a million years would he think that he wouldn't make it home tonight.

"Stay out of sight of them, but not out of sight of you knowing where he going. Ya' feel me?" asked the passenger to the driver that trailed behind Monkey.

"Man, how long we been doing this?" asked the driver with a look of feeling tired.

The passenger smile and shot back, "I know all that. I'm just reminding you, brother-man, that's all."

"Well, if you would have done yo' simple homework then this would be a piece of cake. Plus, this yo' family, so I find it unbelievable you don't know his spot. Consider the shit we popped off for him." The driver told Monkey's uncle, and he knew the words coming from him were true, but Monkey wasn't the same old Monkey people was used to.

He had with him now power and plenty of money to control people with, and he wasn't sucker nigga shit control. He actually fucked with niggas and bitches the correct way, but if you fucked up or over him then you were cut off, and that's what his uncle was.

Two years ago, when Monkey went into big business, he embraced his uncle first. Kash had given Monkey 100 kilos on Gangsta's word, and as promised Monkey broke bread with his uncle, giving him two free kilos and began to front him the bricks for a good price.

The dope came fast and the money came faster, but Monkey's uncle wasn't the hustle type and neither was his two buddies. They messed the money up by being reckless and just wasn't as serious as Monkey was. His uncle messed up three bricks and he had given him another chance after cutting him off for a month. But he fucked up again, this time with $250,000 and some weed. Monkey just cut ties with him through mere love and paid for all losses.

Greed and hate was more powerful than real love. His uncle had turned completely envious of his nephew, and when Monkey cut ties he couldn't take it.

"Well, the man don't fuck with me like that, so we gon' roll up old school and swift, just how we do," Monkey's uncle finally said, because if he could snatch him up he could get to the safe—the big stash. *Fuck Monkey*, was his everyday thought as he lived the normal Westside life, and Monkey lived on the high horse.

"I'm ready," said the driver.

"Yea, me too."

Jerry Jackson

Chapter 10
Pimp

Between her legs, he entered two fingers and pressed down as he slowly licked and sucked her clit. As always, she rotated her hips and kindly held his head in one place as she fed him wet pussy. Every time Pimp stopped pressing down, he would flick his tongue fast over her clit. Just as he started to apply pressure, he would slowly suck it.

He had come home and they instantly started making wild love. She had no chance to question him. He had no chance to peep her move. Pimp had been missing her like crazy and Icey felt the same, so neither could help falling into the bedroom.

Pimp pulled his fingers out of her wetness and began to just softly rub her pussy with the palm of his hand, with applied pressure. He then kissed his way up her stomach and to her breasts, which were extra sensitive. He knew this so he just kissed her neck.

Icey found his hanging dick with her free hand and placed it at her pussy's opening. She gasped for air when he entered her tightness. He felt so good. It was just something about being in love with a man and his hot dick. She closed her eyes tight and went with his flow as he started doing his job. His dick was coated with her pussy juice and cum. She was so warm as he slipped in and out of her. Pimp deep-stroked his girl, holding just one of her legs back by her breast. He knew she was pregnant so he was careful though aggressive.

Pimp kissed her deeply as he stroked the pussy. Pussy so good he had to hold his nut back because it was about to happen. He let her leg go and fell flat on her as Icey started fucking his dick back. He began sucking her earlobe and neck as he grinded into her walls.

"Oh, baby. I love you so, so much," she moaned as he put in his work.

"I love you, too."

Pimp then raised up and looked down at her pretty pussy. He kept stroking her but now he kindly rubbed her hooded clit. He used the bed and its motion to rock her back and forth, sliding up and down his dick.

"Like that, baby. Like that." Icey moaned loud and reached out to scratch his chest.

Pimp kept up that pace and held one of her pretty feet while doing so. "Shit, girl."

"Yes, baby. This dick. Yes, it's so. Oh, baby. It's so goooooooood."

Icey had reached out and grabbed him around the neck as she began to cum. He went deeper into her and grinded as she worked her cum up and down his hard dick. Icey grabbed his face when she had come. She kissed him deeply and started rotating her hips to milk his dick of its cum.

Pimp pulled out of her and turned her over onto her stomach. She was just so sexy. Even from the back she had it going on. He entered her wetness with a deep dive which made her moan and bury her face into the pillow. She lifted her head when he pulled out.

"Don't run."

"It's big, baby—"

"I know." He went deep again. Taking her breath, he pulled back and quickly fell inside her and stayed. "I love how you feel under me."

"Baby, its big. Take some out," Icey plead with her man, looking over her shoulder.

He kissed the side of her face and pulled some of his dick out. He started stroking her kind of hard but not deep. "Like that?" he asked softly.

"Yes, baby, just like that," she replied moaning.

They continued to make love through the wee hours of the night. Icey was loving the feeling of Pimp being home and safe with her wrapped in her arms. This was all any girl wanted, wasn't it? Pimp was in love like no other. He had met no other woman like her in his life and he planned to never let this woman go.

He was feeling his nut about to cum, so he stopped stroking her and laid down on her, preventing her from moving. Also, he started kissing her ear and the back of her neck.

"I love you, baby. I'm 'bout to cum. You want me to cum?" Pimp asked then pulled his dick completely out of her. He slapped her pussy a few times with his dick head.

This gesture made Icey arch her back and reply through a long moan, "Yessssss."

He entered her again and placed his hand at the small of her back, holding him in place, but he didn't go too deep because he knew she couldn't take it like that.

"Shit, girl." He pushed up in her.

"Pull out. Come here," Icey said, turning her body, making his dick slip out.

Pimp stood up and walked to the side of her bed. She got up also and slid off the bed down to her knees. She took his dick and put it in her mouth. It was so warm when her lips and tongue touched his dick. Pimp started rolling his hips and nearly stood on his toes. She took him as far as she could into her throat before she gagged.

Pimp put a hand behind her neck and fucked her mouth; his dick inching more and more into her throat. She gagged and pulled back, nearly throwing up. She squeezed his dick at the base and looked up before putting it back in her mouth.

"I'm 'bout to cum, baby," Pimp said as the feeling of his cum crept through him.

"I want to taste it, baby," Icey said and started sucking his dick head.

Pimp pushed into her mouth again and started fucking her throat.

She gagged again and again and pushed him back. "I can't take it, baby, it's too big," she said, but Pimp was about to cum so he pulled her head back to his hard dick. She allowed him, but this time she held half his dick as he started fucking her mouth again.

This time he was moaning. "Shit, baby. Suck this dick, girl. Shit, baby. Lord have mercy on. Shit, baby." Pimp could not hold it any longer. "Ugh!"

When the first cum hit the back of her throat, she pulled his dick out but kept her mouth open to receive his juice. It was thick and white as it poured over her tongue. Pimp was on the tips of his toes as he jacked-off into her mouth. Once he was done, Icey started draining him by sucking the head only. Pimp jumped from the sensation but didn't run. Icey still held his dick as she looked up to the man she loved and swallowed his load.

Chapter 11
Monkey

Monkey was laid back in the comfort of his Porsche Cayenne Turbo that was bullet proof as it road the highway, getting him home where he belonged. He was partied out. He had drunk enough and smoked enough, now all he was about to do was fuck both the strippers and put them out.

He had a pool house in Buckhead he would take the strippers to because it was a no-no taking anyone to his main spot. Plus, this pool house was used to entertain and grant a level of comfort. It was a place where he did nothing but enjoy himself, so it was nothing to it but to go there tonight.

Monkey made it his business to never show people where he and his family lived because he knew niggas were stupid. Plus, he did great by keeping the streets away from his kids. He was outstanding at being a boss in the streets and a great father at home. Only the important people knew where he laid his head. The pool house was just one of the many spots he had where he did different things. He never brought drugs to the house. It was just a kick back spot for him. The area was laid back in a low-key spot.

Looking to his left and right he saw both the strippers texting on their phones, both on Instagram like every young, bad female. Lustful thoughts invaded his mind as he reached out to the thick one, touching her soft thigh, gaining her attention. "Yo' ass first," he jokingly said and turned to the other one. "You now." He leaned over and kissed the side of her face.

The girl smiled but kept on with her Instagram.

Monkey was about to murder these two lil' hoes tonight with no problems, he thought. He just didn't know he was being tracked by the jack boys. He, nor his security, paid attention to the car that was far behind them. He kept playing with the strippers as the whip made its way off the highway.

The rich and famous lifestyle was more than he could imagine. He was glad he was a hustler and that he ran into Gangsta. This was the best move he could've made in his life and he was happy about it. Monkey had made plenty of money and pulled his entire family out of the struggle. He also helped the streets.

"I hope you got something to drink in there 'cause this Molly got me thirsty as hell," the thick girl said. She was the pretty one but didn't really know it, and that by itself made her cute.

"It's whatever in my spots. You must've forgot who you with?" Monkey said, boasting his status.

"Gots to know. I know," the dark girl quickly shot back. She had put her phone down, looking at Monkey. He could tell she was ready to say she fucked a boss.

"Who don't know you, boy?" the thick one added.

"Well, anything y'all want, y'all can get simple and plain when you with a real nigga."

It took them another twenty minutes to make it to the nice house that sat down a hill. The home was built from stone. It was two stories high with a beautiful front yard of deep green grass. It had cameras everywhere around the house and a high-level security system. The Porsche pulled into the long, downhill driveway and slowly made its way toward the house. As they approached, side lights came on and the cameras locked in on the motion of the whip.

Monkey got out after the thick one and stretched from just sitting there. He had his Glock on him, plus his driver gave him a AR-15 for extra protection, because when Monkey got with his females he always let security go after making sure he was safely inside the spot.

He put the Glock in his pocket, grab his money bag which had $50,000 inside, then held the rifle down by his side as they all made it to the door. He used his key on two locks and was inside with the strippers and his security.

"Man, I got to piss," security said while locking the door behind him.

Monkey punched the code in without even thinking that it reactivated the security on the house.

"Say no mo'. I'm 'bout to roll up. That liquor over at the bar, baby," Monkey said and pulled his gun out, placing it on the coffee table.

The thick girl went straight to the bar.

He saw how fat her ass was in the jeans she wore. "You might as well take them motherfucking pants off," he added pushing the AR-15 under the sofa. He then pulled the cash out the bag and sat it on the table in front of the dark skin girl. She was black and pretty with a slim body and bubble booty.

Monkey saw how she eyed the racks and he walked off, leaving it there. He went into one of the bedrooms, making sure it was the room he wanted to use. The bed was a soft king that he could have some major fun in, but he decided against that room. He walked down the hall as his security was coming out of the bathroom.

"I'm out of here, bro. Happy birthday, my nigga. Smash for me too," security said in passing.

"Okay, bro. Drive that bitch safly," replies Monkey, and found the perfect room where his threesome should take place. He liked the big room because it had an amazing view of the pool with beautiful lights that dimmed to the moment. Monkey smiled and began to strip down so that he could get fresh and clean before he went these rounds with the strippers.

He walked into the bathroom and cut the shower on, sticking his hand under the water, checking its temperature. The slim stripper walked in behind him.

"Can I get in?" she asked and began taking her clothes off, not giving him a choice.

He just smiled and stepped into the water, still watching her sexy ass. His dick started getting hard just looking at the young tender. She was finer than he thought with sexy tattoos.

"You need to hurry up, sexy ass." He encouraged her which made her smile and make her way over to him.

She instantly took his semi-hard dick in her mouth. She rolled her tongue over its head and then grabbed him and start jacking him and sucking at the same time. It felt good to feel her mouth and see the spit that sucking his dick made. She kept at this pace until Monkey started going deeper in her mouth by force, past the point where she wanted him.

She stood up, still holding his dick. She stepped in the shower, dropped to a squat and took him back into her warm mouth. This time she let him fuck her face since her mouth was wetter than it had ever been. His dick slipped back and forth between her lips and she choked a bit when his dick would slide down here throat.

It didn't take long for the other stripper to find them and join the party. "Wow, y'all already started the party without a bitch." She had a glass in her hand. She sat it down on the counter top and began to take her clothes off.

"Nawl, baby, I was just getting fresh. Let's take this shit to the room." Monkey had to stop her because he didn't want to fuck two hoes in the bathroom.

Without hesitation the slim one and thick one went to the room. He followed with a hard dick swinging as he walked.

"Come're. Let me taste that big motherfucker," the thick one said as soon as he stepped over the threshold. She dropped to her knees.

He put the dick right into her mouth. A new mouth was new heat which made him raise up on his toes. The slim girl got behind her and started eating her out as she sucked his dick. This was a sight to see and a feeling to feel. He had plenty of threesomes but it was something about these two young hoes that he couldn't put his hands on. He knew he was going to enjoy the most of it and talk about it later with his partners.

Monkey fucked her mouth good and slow, holding her under the chin and the back of the head. He fed her dick. Her soft, wet lips felt so good wrapped around his dick. Shit was so lovely at the moment, he pushed his dick further into her mouth and down her throat.

"Suck dis dick, hoe," he demanded and held her face so that she couldn't run like she was trying to.

"Ummh." She moaned with a mouthful of dick, plus the sensation of being ate out was added pleasure.

Monkey pulled his hardness away from her mouth. He then climbed into the massive bed. Both girls followed him and started sucking his dick together. Shit felt so good that all he could do was close his eyes and let the king feeling run through him.

The three of them were so in tune with each other that they were totally caught off guard when the door came crashing in to his room and gunmen were what he saw. He was caught and couldn't do shit about it. The first dude came through the door aiming and the second one came in with action by hitting Monkey across the face with his gun.

"Get the fuck down!" the first one said and his partner started with the beating.

"Bitch, shut up!" one of them yelled and struck one of the strippers. The blow was so hard that it knocked her out and created a large cut on her face that instantly started bleeding.

The next stripper panicked when seeing what happened to her friend. She screamed louder.

"Bitch, shut the fuck up!" Monkey heard one of them say.

He was down on one knee with his head bleeding, mad at himself because both his guns were up front. *How did these niggas get in here*, was the next thought he had. They wore masks on their faces so chances were they just wanted some money. As soon as Monkey began to stand up, he was grabbed.

The girl was still screaming which made the other dude aim his gun at her. "Please!"

"Bitch, shut up and get over here!"

"Please, just let me—"

BOOM-BOOM! Two loud shots killed her instantly.

"Fuck!" one of the robbers yelled. "What you did that for, stupid nigga?"

"Man, fuck her! Let's go."

They pulled a limp Monkey toward the front. He wanted to try something but both these niggas had guns and he knew they would use them. His mind was racing, and at the same time he was trying to figure out the voice he heard. Monkey had to hear him speak again to see if it was his uncle.

His head was hurting and blood blinded him, making it hard to see as they pulled him up front. He knew the gun was on the table but when he walked in, he didn't see it. *How did they get in here?*

Was this shit a set up by his security? Was this some kind of inside job? If it was his uncle, then the situation changes.

All he had in the pool house was $50,000 in a bag. That was all the money they would get from him here and no drugs. They pulled him but Monkey acted like he lost his balance and fell in front of the sofa.

He grabbed his head and rocked back and forth. "What's up, man? I got cash. What y'all niggas want?"

"Get yo' ass up! Show us where that safe at," the robber said. He was a skinny dude with dreads under his masked face. The other mask men were exactly the size of his uncle, and that was the voice he wanted to hear.

"Man, ain't no safe in here. That shit at the trap house," Monkey said and wished like hell they would take him anywhere near his squad. "Y'all niggas can have that shit. Half a mill and four bricks." He made it sound sweet. He was still holding his head, acting hurt. He wondered if the AR-15 was loaded to shoot. He had one chance, one shot to get his hand on the gun. He had to make it count.

"Nigga, it's some money in here." The one he wanted to speak had spoken and he confirmed that it was his uncle.

Monkey could not believe it was him. How could this dude cross him? "Bro, I got bricks at the spot and a lil' over half a mill, but not here, my nigga." He continued to play hurt, trying to buy some time. He looked around at the door and didn't see any forced entry which had him thinking crazy.

"Nigga, you going with us! We gonna have yo' bitch pay for yo' life 'cause you want to play pussy, nigga!" The robber hit him again with the gun. "Fuck nigga, stop playing with me!"

Monkey fell down, making sure to reach one hand under the sofa.

"Hold up, hold up, man! Okay, you got it!" He begged just to continue to buy time to check the rifle and make sure the safety was off.

"Get yo' ass up, nigga!" His uncle began to snatch him up.

Monkey let his body weight go, making it harder to move him. He knew that if he didn't act now then it may just be too late for him. With his hand still on the rifle, he turned his head to see where both dudes were. "Hold up, bro, I can't—"

It seemed as everything happened so slow and without volume but at the same time fast. His uncle pulled him up again, but when Monkey came up he pulled with him the AR-15 with one hand.

"Fuck you doin'!"

Shots rang out rapidly. Two, three kind of shots. Monkey knew he had been hit. He could feel the bullets busting him open. He still aimed and took out the shorter one. Monkey couldn't hear the shots or even feel the gun blazing but he could see the large flame and see the body rocking as bullets tore through him.

Monkey knew it was over with for his own life because the first shot to him was his head. He was just so determined to strike at least one of them. The dude managed to get his shots on as well but it was the gunshot wound to the head that killed Monkey.

He wanted to shoot his uncle as he ran out the door but life was leaving his body and he fell face-first to the carpet. Monkey's soul was moving but his mind was somewhat still there. He still couldn't believe his uncle, and he really couldn't believe he was the one that murdered him.

Jerry Jackson

Chapter 12
Pimp

Pimp thought he was tripping when he heard the faint shot of gun-shots in the still of the night. Icey was knocked out and so was he, but he was street and very on point. He sat up slowly and quiet so that he could hear the shots again, not knowing where they came from. It made him grab his own gun out the side draw.

He eased over to the video monitor. It was 6 screens showing outside angles of his home. He hit a button and the view switched to the inside of the house, and he still didn't see anything out of place. So, he walked to his windows and looked out, but again he saw nothing.

The area was very low on crime and it was almost five in the morning. What was someone doing shooting? Pimp was happy that Icey didn't hear the shots, that she was sleep because that's the last thing he wanted. He moved out here for a reason. He had thought this was low-key area.

Pimp closed his curtain back because shit looked normal. He double-checked the monitor and saw the same thing. Maybe he was tripping himself and just was thinking too hard. Maybe he was dreaming, woke and didn't realize it. He walked back to his bed about to get in. he put the gun back in place and that's when he heard a session of different shots.

He went to the window and looked out again and that's when he saw someone emerge from the house next door. The dude was moving fast. A large dude with a mask on. He jumped into a white and blue Cadillac, pulled the mask from his face and pulled off just as quickly.

Pimp wondered what had happened as he shut the curtain back and looked to Icey who was still asleep. He was glad she didn't wake up. *What was going on out here* was his next thought, because it wasn't adding up. It had to be something serious because dude had on a mask. It was real gunshots Pimp heard. It was nothing fake about that.

Back in the bed, he cuddled with Icey. He didn't want her to even know things of such nature taking place in their neighborhood, let alone right under their noses.

Icey was warm to the touch. She inhaled deeply as he got closer. When she exhaled, she slightly moaned, "Love you."

"Love you too, baby," Pimp replied and kissed the back of her neck.

she fell fast asleep but Pimp was left to his own thoughts. He laid there until the sun started to peek and then he heard the police sirens coming, but his eyes were getting heavy. Being tired embraced him again. Pimp closed his eyes as the police got closer. He could hear them coming.

***

When Icey opened her eyes, it was about 7AM and Pimp was knocked out. She smiled at him and their last night's love making. He made her feel so loved and secure when he was around her. She got up out the bed and found the bathroom where she first sat down to pee.

Next, she brushed her teeth and washed her face, getting herself together because today she planned to get out the house for a couple hours. Icey left the room. Walking downstairs she found the kitchen. She wanted something to eat but was too lazy to fix anything and plan to tell Pimp to hire cooks. When she walked toward the refrigerator, she had to pass the window that overlooked the front yard, and that's when she saw so many police officers and patrol cars. Crime scene tape surrounded the entire house that was full of action.

Icey wondered what had happened. She saw a body being brought out the house on a scratcher. It was a woman. Her face was wrapped. She was barely naked as the medic's rush to the awaiting ambulance. Shortly after that, Icey saw a body bag being brought out the house and heard a scream from a woman in the crowd. People had to hold the woman back. She had to be family. Icey was in total disbelief as she watched the house next door.

Pimp said it was safe. He promised her safety, didn't he? Looking still, she saw two more body bags being brought out. She had lost her appetite. She could not eat anymore. She couldn't look anymore. She ran upstairs to wake Pimp up. She was scared.

"Baby!" She walked into their room and snatched the curtain back. "Look, baby! Three people dead next door! Look," she said, which made Pimp wake up and roll over toward her.

"Huh?" he questioned, looking up.

"Get up and look, baby," Icey demanded.

Pimp did as he was told. She didn't know he knew something had happened last night. Pimp came over and pulled her into his arms. He kissed the side of her face and looked out the window to see what he knew she was talking about. "Wow. I wondered what happened," Pimp said, because he didn't know and he wanted to know himself what went on so close to his house.

"That truck there got three bodies inside." She pointed. A news crew was out there and so was the entire neighborhood, to see what was going on.

Pimp pulled her from the window. "Baby, I'm gonna move us if need be. Just say the words." Pimp meant it.

"I'm just scared, baby," she admitted honestly.

He hugged her tight again. "Don't be. You have no reasons," Pimp assured her. He knew if she had saw what he thought, it would be an uphill battle trying to convince her it was cool.

Icey wanted to believe the words of Pimp but she could not help the fear she felt. She could not help the doubt she held. It was like trouble followed Pimp everywhere he went.

"I'm hungry," Icey said.

"Me too. Get dressed. Got a place you'll like." Pimp made her stand up. It was a good idea to get her out the house.

Icey went into her closet and Pimp got up to get dressed also. He would take her to have fun today, show her that Atlanta wasn't always about killing and drug dealing.

Jerry Jackson

Chapter 13
Trish

Veedoo and Trish were eating breakfast the next morning when she had gotten the call from one of the agents about a very good lead on the investigation of the bombing.

"Excuse me, baby. I need to take this call," she told her husband and got up from the table with the phone glued to her ear.

Veedoo nodded and continued to eat his steak and eggs with cheese grits.

Trish walked into another room in their home and pulled the door up. "Yes? Agent Williams here."

"Ma'am, I have a man demanding federal protection for information about the bombing. He's in my office right now and it seems he knows what he's talking about," the agent said into the phone.

"Federal protection must follow guidelines, and the intel we receive must be accurate. We must also confirm," Trish told him. She knew all the rules about her job. That's why she was top of her class.

"Yes. That's why I called you, because it sounds about like this could lead to something, but I know you are the expert in this type of stuff."

"And he's in the office now?" asked Trish. She wanted to know if she had heard him correctly.

"Yes. Right here," he answered.

This made her wonder what this dude had that was so important. Today was supposed be spent with her husband, starting with breakfast then an outing. Not waking up to work, but it did sound very important.

Trish closed her eyes. She took a deep breath and shook her head before she spoke into the phone.

"Okay, listen. Put him in a holding cell for a few hours and I'll be there by one to see if I can even ask the judge to sign off on federal protection."

"Yes. ma'am. I'm on it."

"Okay, text me when he's in place." Trish had to remind him so he wouldn't forget. She hung up the phone and walked back into the kitchen where Veedoo sat eating. She kissed his head in passing to get to her seat and also began eating.

"Everything good, baby?" Veedoo asked after drinking orange juice from his cup.

"Yes, just the job. I'm not gonna be able to make it on our little date, baby." Trish hated to admit it but she had to.

"What you mean?" He sounded pissed.

She knew he was pissed. "Something extremely important came up, baby, but I can make it up though. Right now, make it up."

She knew Veedoo would be mad, that's why she set the time to 1PM because she had planned to seduce him with their love making in exchange for standing him up. Veedoo just looked at his wife from across the table. Trish was as beautiful as ever. He loved this fact. Every day he awoke to someone so amazing.

She stood up from her seat. She came toward him so he too stood up. She never took her eyes off his as she approached, until she was in his arms.

They kissed deeply. Veedoo gripped her booty. She had both hands on either side of his face. He pulled her kind of close. He rubbed her booty and squeeze it as he tongued her down.

Trish then grabbed him around the neck and stood on her toes. "I'll meet you in the room."

Veedoo let her go after the kiss and patted her soft booty as she walked off.

She looked back to see him grab his crotch and bite his lip lustfully at his wife. She loved it when he did that. She smiled and went her way to their bedroom.

Veedoo went to his laptop to send an important email and invoice real quick for a business project in Alaska for a contract. Afterward, he also sent an authorization code to the trucking company owned by Gangsta to open some cargo containers.

Trish was only in her bra when he entered the room. Her body was so sexy and in shape that it made no sense. She was beautiful. She was bad. Veedoo went straight at his wife, pushing her to lay back because she was already sitting down on the bed. He spread her legs far apart and kissed her pussy lips sideways.

72

The instant touch of his lips to her moist middle made her jump. She moaned when she felt his tongue slide between her pussy lips, going back and forth making her moist pussy wet now. Trish couldn't help but to lift her hips up and grab the top of his head. Veedoo then circled her clit with his tongue. He used his hand to pull her hood back, exposing her protruding clit. This made her push his head instead of grab it because it gave her a new sensation she wasn't expecting.

Veedoo kept going though she was trying to run. Moving his head from side to side he kept sucking her pussy and holding one leg open one hand on her stomach.

"Lord, baby. Shit. Eat this pussy, boy. Eat this pussy," Trish said as she rotated her hips into his mouth, looking him in his eyes as he looked at her. She was in a trans; in a zone and about to cum.

He pressed down on her stomach and slipped two fingers into her pussy. He sat up and she put one of her legs on his shoulder. Veedoo started fucking her pussy with force but slowly as she continued to roll her hips. "You like that?" He circled and dug into her pussy.

"Yes!" she cried in pure pleasure.

He then pulled his fingers from her, stood up and pulled his dick out. He was rock hard and ready to dive into her tightness. He got comfortable between her legs and entered her walls. "Ah, shit. Yes." Veedoo moaned, feeling her warm pussy wrapped around his dick. He went deep into her.

"Ummh." Trish felt him near her guts.

He started grinding into her, going in and out of her wet pussy at a nice pace. It felt so good that she closed her eyes and locked her mind on the feeling that had her in heaven.

Veedoo took one of her legs by the ankle and opened it wider. He was standing up while half her body hung off the bed. He went deeper with his stroking, making her reach out to him and beg him to stop.

"Slow down, baby. Take some out," she managed to moan.

Veedoo pulled completely out of her and pulled her to stand up. Then, he turned her around and pushed her to lay her chest on the bed as he got comfortable and slid into her from the back.

"Yes, baby, yes!" she moaned loudly and put her face into the bed as he started thrusting into her. He slapped her butt and gripped it as he worked her over. "Oh my Gooo-God!"

If she wanted to run, she couldn't because he had her locked in with her feet planted on the floor. All she was able to do was reach out and grab at the sheets and covers. He held her at the hip and thigh, making her rock back and forth on his dick. He put the palm of his hand on the middle of her back. Her lower back. Bending his knees just a little, he started beating the pussy good. Trish moaned in pleasure and tried desperately to run. She couldn't go anywhere though.

Veedoo would not stop either because the pussy was good and he was near cumming inside his wife like always. With a few more strokes he laid over her back and kissed her ear as he came inside her hard with grinds and grunts. "I love you, baby," he said as he came.

"I-I love you too, baby! Yes, baby," Trish spoke over her shoulder as she came, also making it magical.

Chapter 14
Gangsta

Gangsta was just getting out the bed when Junior walked into the room, followed by Loco and Meco. Both guys had tired looks in their eyes and both still had on the clothes from last night.

"Monkey got murdered, my friend." Loco was the first to speak.

"Junior, step out," Gangsta told his son and sat up. He couldn't believe what he just heard. "What happened?" he calmly asked, looking at both his friends.

"Nigga followed him home. He killed one of the men but got popped himself along with two stripper hoes. One made it. One didn't," Meco said.

"Who is the dead one? Anyone know yet?" Gangsta asked.

"My people are working on all intel as of now 'cause we are at a loss," Loco said

"What about the stripper? She got to know something."

"Yeah, but police got protection at the hospital right now. We got to wait until she gets home," Loco answered.

"Okay, did they get anything?" Gangsta wanted to know. His mind was trying to process what had happened. Monkey was a real true friend in his eyes. He took this very, very personal. Not only was it disrespectful, it hurt like hell to lose someone you came to love as family. Since the day he had met Monkey he had been solid to him and it was all love. To hear that he was murdered last night on his birthday was painful at the thought. Gangsta started getting dressed.

"Nawl. Fuck niggas didn't get one penny, one bomb. He was at the pool house in Buckhead, not his home-home though," Meco answered.

Gangsta put on the same clothes from last night and he got his phone and ID before going into the restroom. He spent the next five minutes rushing with brushing his teeth and washing his face. He met up with his friends downstairs.

Ne-Ne was cooking breakfast when Gangsta made it to the kitchen. Loco and Meco stood at the door.

"Baby, I'll miss breakfast. I'll call you in a few to let you know what's going on, but Monkey got hurt last night." Gangsta leaned in and kissed his wife.

Ne-Ne returned the kiss but gave a skeptical look to him. "Don't go out there acting young, baby," she reminded him and they kissed once again.

"Never that, baby," Gangsta assured her. He knew his limits in the streets.

She knew it too but she was just being concerned because she knew her husband.

Outside, Loco had a bullet proof truck waiting on them. Security rode in a opposite car with only one marksman riding with them.

"Where Kash?" Gangsta got seated beside Loco.

"He was at Monkey's sister's place. That's where we headed now because she's the one who knows everything."

Since Gangsta escaped prison, he had spent precious time getting him and his team in a good position. It took sacrifice and blood to get to the point where everyone was working with each other. Gangsta and his team had the drug trade in Atlanta running like the rap game. Any nigga who went against them felt the pain, and most niggas respected it and got with the program.

He couldn't understand. For the past two years shit had been Gucci, and all of a sudden some fuck shit happens out of nowhere, and to a good nigga. Someone had to answer to this with their life and life of those they love, too. He was pissed off as the truck hit the highway, headed to Monkey's sister crib. Gangsta couldn't wait to get there to see what was really going on so he could handle it fast. This shit was personal.

"Where was his security?" Loco asked this question out of nowhere and to no one in particular.

"Yeah, didn't he leave with security? That's the big question," Meco added

"As always," Gangsta said because he knew Monkey never went anywhere without at least one security member. It was a rule they had to stick with in order to make it as far as they have made it in this game. Niggas hated, even when you helped them so it's obvious that niggas will kill you about what they hate you for.

It took them 45 minutes to get out to Monkey's sister's crib. She stayed in Lithonia, Georgia in a nice neighborhood. Cars and trucks filled the yard, preventing them from parking so they found a spot in front of the large home that was beautifully decorated.

Once out the truck, Gangsta and his crew were greeted by Monkey's sister's best friend. She gave all the guys sorrowful hugs then led them into the house.

"Come on. She's barley making it through this," the best friend spoke over her shoulder. She led way through the house that held fairly a large group of people gathering around.

They followed her up the steps and found Monkey's sister and another woman sitting down. Both appeared shaken up. Both had been and still was crying.

At first, she wouldn't look up, but then when hearing Monkey's name she looked up to the face of Gangsta—a person she knew through her brother.

"What's up, Mekka?" Gangsta spoke to her.

"Hey." She got up and walked into his embrace.

Gangsta felt the same as hurt. She wasn't in this alone. They walked off to talk in private.

"What happened, Mekka?"

Monkey's sister she took a deep breath and thought long before speaking. She was still trying to be strong. She was about to break down like she'd been doing all morning. She looked at Gangsta. "They got surveillance. They got my brother being killed on tape." Mekka broke down crying. She couldn't help it.

Gangsta pulled her into his embrace.

Kash was walking from the back of the house. He had with him a heavy duffle bag filled with cash. "Did the police tell you how the killers got in?" Kash just asked anyone who had an answer.

"Kicked the door in," she replied through cries.

"Thought I told everyone to make sure they secure before security leave us?" Gangsta said while looking at Kash for answers.

"I got his security on the way over now to explain what the hell happened, 'cause it's an alarm system that was shut off and not active," Kash explained

"They shot him eleven times." Mekka broke down again.

"You gonna be okay, Mekka. I promise, shawty," Gangsta said only to her. He knew she needed strength right now, no matter what.

"The bitch who at the hospital I know from the strip club, but the dead nigga I never seen, and he an older nigga," Kash added and his phone started ringing. "Hold on, this Veedoo." Kash took the call while Gangsta continued to console Mekka for the loss of her brother.

Monkey was her rock. He was the family's Superman and someone took him away from her. Gangsta felt her and his own pain as he tried to push thoughts about Monkey from his mind to stay strong for not only himself but for the team as well.

"What's up with Veedoo?" Gangsta asked because he noticed a crazy look on Kash's face as he listened to whatever Veedoo was talking about.

At first Kash held up a finger but then he pulled the phone from his ear and put it on speaker phone. "Shawty, say that again. I got Gangsta right here. You on speaker," Kash then said.

"Man, I told Monkey last night it was some niggas in the cut, watching his movements. Bro brushed it off like it was good. Plus, I know how he rock with security so I left. But, yeah, I pulled shawty coattail on that situation," Veedoo explained to Gangsta but everyone listened.

"Did you get a good look at anyone of them niggas?" Gangsta hoped like hell he said yes.

"They was in the cut. All I could tell was that they was some older cats."

"We was there. Do you remember seeing any old niggas?" Kash asked.

"Only old people outside our age range was my uncle and his friends who's like our uncle, and he wouldn't do no shit like that," Mekka stated. She just knew her family was close-knit.

"We can get surveillance pulled at the club for a nice check," Loco finally cut in with some good ideas of what could've happened.

It sounded about right to Gangsta because they were plugged in with most of the club owners in Atlanta. "You right," said Gangsta with a nod.

"Man, when I left that motherfucker, y'all was still in the parking lot. I just had told Monkey that shit and he still slipped. I felt that shit, bro," Veedoo stressed through the phone.

"Okay, say less, bro. I'll get up with you later on," Gangsta told Veedoo as his mind raced to put this situation together. Something wasn't right and he vowed to find out what it was.

Jerry Jackson

Chapter 15
Pimp

Pimp and Icey had breakfast at the White House— a breakfast restaurant that was banging with some of the best food money could buy. Icey just had a simple pancake breakfast with sausage and bacon wrapped around cheese sticks. Pimp did waffles, scrabbled eggs and cheese grits. Pimp was looking at his beautiful, pregnant girl as she killed her food.

Icey hadn't said anything since the food arrived. She just attacked the plate. Pimp could only smile because she did say she was hungry and he knew she was pregnant. She was eating the cheese stick when she finally looked up to find Pimp looking directly at her. She burst into laughter and so did Pimp.

"Why are you looking at me like that, baby?" she asked, still laughing.

"You full yet, baby?" He smiled while eating his own food.

"Almost." She smiled too.

Pimp was only trying to take her mind off the bullshit she witnessed this morning. He was doing good so far, and by the end of the day he planned to have her fully captivated by fun and love.

"I love you, woman." Pimp got soft and serious, and she did too.

"I love you, man."

"You better." He was happy he met this woman. She just didn't know it.

They sat there another twenty minutes talking and joking until the food got cold. Pimp was walking behind her as they left the restaurant. The last person or people he expected to see was Montay and his lil' homies rolling up on him early in the morning.

"Whoa! Wazham, foo? What's mobbing?" one of the GF members approached.

Then, Montay showed his face. "Pimp, what's good, bro?" Montay waved to Icey for respect then turned his attention back to Pimp. "One of my good friends got popped last night."

As soon as Montay said the words, Pimp thought about his neighbor. He most definitely hoped he wasn't talking about the shit that happened last night. "Damn. Sorry to hear about that. You straight?" Pimp asked.

"Yeah. Just 'bout to grab something to eat before we head to his spot. Shit fucked up. Nigga got murked on his birthday." Montay shook his head.

"Yeah, that's ugly. But just hit me later, bro. I'll pull up on you," Pimp said because he didn't want Icey to hear too much of the conversation.

Montay caught on to Pimp and thought about his own situation with Icey. "Okay, brother. I'll call in a couple hours," Montay quickly replied.

"Bet."

He again waved at Icey then they went their separate ways. Pimp took his girl's hand and they continued to the car. He had another spot to take her where he knew it would ease her mind.

"How was the food, baby? How are you feeling?" Pimp decided to ask as the headed to the car.

"It was good, to my surprise, 'cause I didn't think I would like it."

"That's what I thought when I first ever ate there, but they're breakfast always banging." He informed her.

They made it to the ride and he opened the door for her. Icey settled in her seat. He leaned inside to kiss her then he did the same to her stomach.

He ran around the ride and hopped in himself. The time was just right to pull up to this place he knew she would love. Pimp crank up and started messing with the radio so he could find his favorite song.

"Now where are we going?" Icey wanted to know because she had plans of her own.

But Pimp only smiled that smile at her and refocus on the road ahead of them. "I love you."

"I don't want to hear that. I want to know where you taking me." Icey laughed then said, "I love you too, but I still wanna know."

"Just trust me, baby," Pimp shot back.

Icey playfully rolled her eyes and sat comfortably in her seat. She was with her man, she was happy to be with him, but she still wanted to go out alone and explore the city herself.

Montay

Montay and two of his GF brothers were following the GPS as it directed them to Monkey's pool house in Buckhead. The music was playing low while all the guys were thinking of what happened and what went down.

This situation to Montay was a wake-up call to him, and even more reason for him to get out the game because Monkey was a good dude and it was messed up how someone took him out the game. Niggas didn't have no respect for the game anymore, or for real niggas. Now, someone was forcing their hands, making them put it in the dirt.

All he wanted was out the game and some much-needed rest from these streets, but it seemed like the game wasn't trying to let him go. It took them twenty minutes to find the pool house and pull into the driveway. Crime scene tape was still all over the place and a few friends and family members were in and around the house. Montay got this eerie feeling once the ride stopped. He felt deja vu of some sort as he just looked at the front door of Monkey's home.

It wasn't until they all stepped out of the ride that Montay got surprised and shocked. So shocked that it was noticed by his GF brothers.

"Fuck going on, foo? You straight?"

"Hell yeah. Just was thinking and shit." Montay eased it off him.

He was stuck, and what he just found out, he would probably have to keep to himself right now because shit was looking crazy.

All the guys proceeded to the house, all the while Montay was looking and confirming that the G wagon in the yard over was Pimp's car. It was Pimp who lived next door.

He knew Pimp's mojo, and the way things were looking, it looked like Pimp's work. Montay kept this to himself. Now he saw why Pimp was so apprehensive to talk to him when they saw him at the restaurant. Now he saw what the deal was and if Pimp thought he would get away from this, he had another thing coming.

Inside the house, Montay and his brothers were led to the back where it was a hidden safe that was strictly for a backup file on the surveillance that was at the house. Gangsta sent him over once they talked to Monkey's sister.

"Fuck you think did this shit?" one GF asked.

"I'on know but I bet we 'bout to find out," Montay replied and began to open the safe.

Montay's mind would not leave the fact that Pimp stayed right next door and was acting strangely. He had to talk to him and do it fast because shit wasn't right. The safe was opened and a tape was extracted from the player. He closed it back. The only people in the room was Montay, his two GF brothers and one of Monkey's family members making sure they didn't take anything else out the house.

Upfront, Montay paid his respect to the sister and Monkey's mother, also with hugs and caring words.

"We will find out what happened. I promise. You and your family will be straight as long as I live. Okay?" Montay said in an embrace with Monkey's mother.

"Okay, baby. Thank you," she replied.

He left with the tapes of Monkey's murder. Inside the whip he sent Gangsta a text letting him know everything was good. Pimp came to his mind once again; something he couldn't shake. One thing was for certain though was the facts were about to be shown and Montay could not wait.

Chapter 16
Brad

Brad was in the office when he got the call he had been expecting from the informant who was the woman from the corner.

She started speaking as soon as he got on the line. "I saw a white van. A man inside got out and went to the back of the funeral home." That was the first thing she said when she got on the phone.

Brad was ecstatic but cautious that this could be just some made up story and not an incredible lead. A lead that the Team needed at the moment.

"Slow down, ma'am. Where did you see a van?" Brad took out a pen and paper and began to write and listen. He didn't want to forget anything.

The woman took a deep breath before going on to say, "The van was parked on the side street, kinda like behind the funeral home." The woman answered but quickly stopped and said, "Isn't it a reward or something for this information?" Almost everyone tried this technique when it came to information given and telling on someone.

"I'm pretty sure it's an award out for the capture of the suspect rather convicted or not, but first thing first, we must see if what you are telling me is the truth," Brad had to inform her but the things she had said so far was better than anything he's heard. He thought it was something to go off of.

"Well, I know what I saw. Matter of fact, I walked around the back and saw him breaking in, but after that I got the hell on 'cause a son of a bitch had to be crazy to break into a fucking funeral home," the woman spoke.

"Did you get the plates on the van?" Brad continue to write.

"Didn't I tell you I got the hell on?"

"I'm just covering all grounds, ma'am. So, what else do you remember?"

"Nothing else. What's up with the information and the money exchange?"

Brad could tell the woman was becoming agitated with his questions, so he asked, "Okay. Can you come into the office so we can go over the proper paperwork?"

"I need a ride if it's not on Northside Drive," she quickly shot back.

"Okay. That can be arranged," Brad said and took down her location so he could have Atlanta police patrol pick her up.

After ending the phone call Brad instantly started going over what he wrote down. He had totally forgotten to ask if she could describe the suspect. How did this guy look? This information is very important.

Brad was kind of excited by this new lead and highly felt strongly enough about it. *Things were already looking good*, he thought as he got up from his desk.

Chapter 17
Pimp

Pimp was on 285 when he exited on Camp Creek Parkway. Icey had never been to Atlanta so everything she saw was new to her. Pimp made a right turn off the highway and continued to drive. She had no idea what he had in store for her. Pimp reached over and rubbed her stomach. They smiled at each other as he eased through traffic.

"'Bout fifteen more minutes," Pimp told her and focused on the road ahead.

Camp Creek Parkway was crowded with traffic, coming and going into many shopping centers. Icey just looked while riding. Pimp finally used his turn signal and soon after made the turn into a large shopping center that was empty in the parking lot. Only one nail salon was open at the end of the building.

Everything else looked like it was being worked on from what Icey could see. Her nails were done already, so what were they doing here rather than some other shopping center was her question.

Pimp, on the other hand, parked the car and with a smile on his face killed the engine before saying, "Come on, baby." Pimp then got out the ride and rushed around to her side to help her out of the car.

"Baby, what's going on?" She was confused but she had to ask while being helped out to the ground.

Pimp continue to hold her hand while leading her toward this empty building. To Icey it could be at least a couple stores in this one area. Pimp pointed to the top of the building where a sign should've been.

"What's the name of your school? You shall put it there. Right there. After construction is done, this will be your school here in Georgia. Keep the same name or change it, but this entire area is yours."

When Pimp said those words, Icey was shocked and in awe of what she saw. *Pimp is amazing*, she thought. She could not believe her eyes as she was seeing this building being brought to life.

"Baby, I don't know what to say." Icey was captivated and he knew and hoped it had this effect on her. He was happy it did.

"Baby, all I want you to say is I love you." Pimp kissed her deeply with passion.

"I love you, baby!" Pimp had just made her day with this one.

"Now, you can have it arranged how you like. All this is yours, baby." Pimp was proud of himself to make this happen.

Icey jumped into his arms again, this time being the aggressive one with their kiss.

Hand and hand they walked into the building for a quick tour. Pimp used the key to enter past the gates, then he used the key to open the door. Once inside the place Icey started looking around with this huge smile on her face. Pimp kind of followed and pulled his phone out to begin texting his father's lawyer to call him.

Pimp had handled the business with the judge in a fashion that will not point to him. Now it shouldn't be a reason to keep his father from another trial. This was the reason Pimp went so hard and chased the money and power. His father's freedom was the reason.

"Baby, this place is larger; twice as big as the one in Miami. Do you know what I can do with this school?" Icey's excitement could not be hidden. It was all over her face, all in her energy. It made Pimp smile.

Icey continued to walk as he followed. It was a text message from Montay saying they needed to meet, and another text from his dad's lawyer saying that she needed him to come into the office. Pimp pocketed the phone because neither Montay nor the freaky ass lawyer was talking about anything right now. All Pimp wanted was to bathe in Icey's joy because boy she was happy.

Just as Pimp got ready to hug his girl from behind, his phone started ringing. He pulled it out and saw that it was the lawyer.

"Ma'am?" Pimp picked up. He still kissed the side of Icey face.

"What I tell you 'bout that, Savarous?" the lawyer spoke.

"Just respect. What's up, though? What's going on?" Pimp wanted to get to the point of the phone call.

"I need to see you in the office," was all she said.

"When? Like, today?"

"Yes. Right now, if possible, but at least before I leave. I really need to see you," she said in a slick manner that Pimp read exactly how she intended for him to take it.

Pimp could only mentally shake his head before he replied. "Okay, I'll be there." And without giving her a chance to reply, he hung up in her face, sending his own slick message, playing the same mind game she was playing.

Jerry Jackson

Chapter 18
Brad

Brad was stuck as he stood there looking at a sketch of a person who resembled Pimp. He was in the office with a federal sketch artist and the witness. Brad could not believe it so he pulled a real-life picture of Pimp out.

When the woman saw it, she jumped up in a for sure manner and pointed. "That's him!"

"You sure?" Brad's heart was in his chest literally.

"Baby, I'm more positive than ever."

Brad took this information to Mrs. Williams who was also was happy with the intel. She sent agents to every van rental place to check and see if this suspect rented a van. She also had agents out looking for any abandoned white vans. This lead seemed promising and this was what they went on.

Brad was given the surveillance job of Pimp and his home. They could only survey him six hours each day. Six hours Brad knew he would love and this time he would not mess the case up. This time he planned to handle it correctly.

He continued to stare at the picture of Pimp and could not believe it. Pimp was some character. Pimp was a mad man that needed to be stopped. Icey was in great danger and she needed to be saved from this man who walked around like he could kill, rob and steal like it was legal.

Something on the inside of Brad wanted this to not be true also, just for the sake of Icey because if it did have any truth to it then Pimp was in more trouble than the first time. This time, it wasn't no getting away.

"So, I helped y'all. Now where is my money? My reward?" the woman asked looking like she was high right then and there.

Brad knew he had to do something and do it fast. "Let me get with my boss. Hold up a second." Brad He didn't want to lose his witness. He walked out of his office and down the hall to Mrs. Williams's office. He softly knocked on the partially open door where a beautiful Mrs. Williams sat behind her desk.

"Come in, agent. What you got?" She greeted him with a professional manner.

He calmly walked in. "The witness I have. She wants to be. She wants us to like, give. She wants to know if it's an award or something." Brad could hardly get out the statement.

"What are you saying, sir?" Mrs. Williams asked.

"She wants to be compensated," Brad said.

"Agent, you know it's extremely against policy to pay or bribe a witness. Where is this woman from? Where does she reside?"

"She lives on the streets. Her and her husband—"

"Sir, explain the meaning of streets," Mrs. Williams cut in.

"I mean exactly how it sounds. She's a bum who sleeps on the streets."

"So, it's safe to say she's a drug addict?" Mrs. Williams wanted to know.

"I'm not sure about all that. I just know she's the only eye witness we have that's willing to work with us. I know it's against policy to pay witnesses for information and I'm not going against policy for no one. I was only asking you for advice. What should I tell her? What should I do?" Brad decided to be up front.

Mrs. Williams sat there in thought for a moment. She just looked at him without one word spoken. She was strictly by the book and did her job to perfection. She could not give in to what this woman wanted, no matter if she had a good story or not. "You can let her go. Tell her the only thing we can do is hold the information until someone offers a reward, but as of right now it's no reward out for information. If it's given, it's just that," Mrs. Williams explained to Brad.

That explanation was good enough for him. He left her office to break the news to the woman that she could not be paid. "Ma'am?"

She was still sitting there with the sketch agent and a uniformed official.

"Unfortunately, we will have to wait on someone to offer up a reward before we could consider the possibility of you getting it."

"What! So, you played me!" The woman's face became beet red as she stood.

Brad knew this would be her reaction. He knew this would leave him in a difficult place to decide what to do. "Calm down, ma'am," Brad urged her.

The uniformed official got closer to the woman so that he could gain some control over her if she got out of hand.

"Calm down! I come in here and help y'all motherfuckas and this the thanks I get!" The lady tried to raise her hand to slap some of the things off Brad's desk, but the uniformed official quickly stopped her.

"Get her out of here," Brad demanded with a point of his finger. He was glad she tried to pull that stunt. It gave him reason to not explain anything to her and to get rid of her. He had enough of her statement to put together whatever he wanted on Pimp. They didn't need her anymore.

Jerry Jackson

Chapter 19
Trish

Trish's mind was captivated with her husband and the sex they had before leaving this morning. It was some amazing sex and she wanted some more.

Squeezing her thighs together under her desk, she was feeling her pussy becoming wet from thoughts of them. With lots and lots of work in front of her, she still managed to find her hand easing down between her legs. Just as she was about to open her legs, her phone rang.

Her eyes quickly opened and the emotion of embarrassment took over. She didn't realize her eyes had been closed. Did anyone see her? How long had her eyes been closed?

She reached out and picked up the phone call. "Special Agent Williams speaking."

"You need to get down to the funeral home." It was another agent.

"What's going on?" She stood up from her desk.

"Got some intel from the owner. He has a possible suspect that came in asking questions. I did a check on the name he said she gave, and it's no such person living with that information," the agent said.

"Did you get a description of her? Can he point her out?"

"Yes. He said he'll never forget her face."

"Okay. I'm on my way over." She grabbed her cell, car keys and gun before shutting down her computer. The case was looking better and better as they went, Trish thought, walking to the elevator.

"Mrs. Williams, glad I caught you." Another case agent approached, holding folded papers in his hand.

"What you have?" Trish took the paperwork and began to read briefly as he spoke.

"Stolen white van recovered approximately sixteen blocks from the church. Get this. The van had bomb making material inside." The agent was happy to repeat the news.

Trish was even more happy but it didn't show. "This is good work. Where is the van?" she asked as the elevator doors opened, and the two walked in.

"It's at the forensic lab being processed."

"Yes, that's good. Has anyone processed the area where the van was found? Has anyone been sent out in search of witnesses?"

"I'm not sure but I will most definitely get on it, ma'am," the agent said and got the paperwork back from her. He was young and new. She could tell as the elevator went down to the parking garage.

"Well, it's always critical to process the crime scene, and checking for eye witnesses is crucial, too." Trish gave the young agent pointers on how to be a great FBI agent.

They got off in the parking lot. She walked to her car and got in. Her mind found its way back to her husband as she crank the car. *This was about to be a very long day*, she thought and pulled off, headed to the funeral home.

Pimp

When Pimp walked into the lawyer's office he immediately saw the disappointment on the lawyer's face when she noticed Icey with him. He knew she would not like this but it was intended to be that way because if it was any other way then it would be him being uncomfortable.

"How are you?" Pimp asked and took Icey's hand.

"I'm good, sir. I called you in to talk to you about your friend Dontae. I can get his entire case tossed."

"How?" Pimp wanted to know.

"The search warrant wasn't dated until after he was arrested."

"What about the condo being in my name?"

"That's another thing. that's not an issue at all. Remember, no warrant, no entrance," the lawyer assured him.

"That's good. What we waiting on then with Dontae?" asked Pimp.

"It will set your father's court date off by a few months because the firm focus must be on Dontae's case."

"The witness is dead, though, so why do y'all gotta work so hard to get him out?"

"'Cause when the FBI gets to you then it's procedures to follow," the lawyer explained.

Pimp was thinking hard for a moment. He and Icey both took seats as his mind raced. "So, if we go at my father first, then what?"

"Then, Dontae will be put off by a couple months."

"Shid. Get my father first. Bra can wait a few months. My pops been in over twenty years."

"Okay, that's fine." The lawyer started writing something down; clearly mad.

Pimp took the time to introduce Icey. "I want you to meet my beautiful wife, Icey. She will be coming to meet with you at times when I'm unable," Pimp said. He knew upon saying it that this would most definitely get under her skin.

Instantly her facial expression changed but her fake smile remained when she looked up and spoke to Icey. "Nice to meet you, ma'am."

"Nice to meet you, too." Icey was equally polite, not knowing the true situation. Not knowing this woman really wanted to fuck her man and really didn't want her in the office.

Pimp smirked mainly to himself as he guided Icey out of the office with him. That should fix the lawyer and all her unwanted advances because it was strictly business with him. He wanted his father home and nothing would get in the way of that.

Outside, he opened the car door for his girl. She got in and reached for the seatbelt.

He grabbed it first and leaned into the car to kiss her. "I love you."

"I most definitely love you," Icey replied and took the seat belt from his hand.

Pimp made his way around to the driver's side. He had one last stop for her and then he had business to handle. He crank the car up, and with one more kiss, he pulled away from the law office.

***

An hour later and a quick bite to eat at Captain D's, Pimp pulled up into an empty parking lot of a grocery store that was vacant.

"Get out, baby." Pimp quickly jumped out and Icey followed.

He took her hand, standing in front of the store. Behind them was a large apartment complex that was also abandoned.

"What's this?" Icey asked, kind of confused.

"All this is mine. This store and them." He turned her around to face the apartments. He purchased the property years ago.

"Wow."

"So, while you running yo' business in College Park, I'll be right here or over there." He pointed to the apartments and kissed the side of her face.

She turned fully in his arms and they shared a very deep and passionate kiss. Both were madly in love with each other.

Pimp was good with how his morning started off with peace. This was something he hadn't had in a long time. He really, really needed to spend time with his girl. His mind could clear up. The last two states he'd been to wore him out tremendously. He wasn't stressing but the pressure from the feds and the beef was too much of the wrong shit. He was being side-tracked from the main objective and he had to quickly get it together. That was another reason he was glad to meet Icey, because she made a difference.

He got away with all the wrong he'd done state to state, and he had plans to stay clear of trouble. He had everything going good for him and his girl. He had a clean slate that he'd take advantage of. Well, least that's what Pimp thought.

"How many apartments over there, baby?" Icey asked, turning back around in his arms to face the complex again.

"It's eighty apartments— twenty four-bedrooms, fifty two-bedrooms and ten singles." He was proud to answer.

"You share this with someone?"

"No. It's all mine."

"Great, baby. This is good." Icey had to admit, she was impressed with this man as every day passed. "I love your mind."

"I love everything about you," Pimp said back. Another kiss and he walked her closer to the store. "I was thinking to open a super Walmart, a barbershop and nail salon, all in this store front."

"I can see it," Icey said as they looked at the store with vision.

Pimp told her about a few more ideas he had, and then he left there and headed home. They were happy and content with each other and how things are going. Icey was happy because she could have her school and her man. Pimp was happy because her mind was clear of the nonsense that surrounded them.

Jerry Jackson

Chapter 20
Trish

Trish pulled up to the funeral home and was met by more field agents and detectives outside in the parking lot.

The first man to approach her briefed her on what was going on. "We set up a perimeter around the entire block, going door to door, business to business, home to home. We also obtained surveillance from a store behind the funeral home that's being processed now. So far we have one witness and no likely suspects," the agents said as they walked inside the funeral home.

"Good work, sir," she told the agent and came face to face with the owner of the place. Trish offered her hand in a shake. "Hello, I'm special agent Williams." She also flashed her ID badge to him.

"I've met many of you in the past two days. How are you today?" The old white man showed equal respect.

"Understood. Listen, I need you to repeat the events of yesterday for me so I too can have a clear picture," Mrs. Williams stated because she did not want to miss anything.

"Listen, I don't mind telling you everything I know, it's just that I got to have a cup of coffee. I hadn't had one all day."

Trish felt where he was coming from. She too needed a hot cup of coffee. "Yes. No problem, sir."

While he walked away to fix his coffee she took the time to walk around the place to look for anything that would point to the bomber or any possible leads. FBI agents were all over the place as she made her way through. Trish found herself downstairs in the basement and prep room. Crime scene technician were processing the area around a window that had to be the entrance point. Trish noticed, when she looked up by the window, she saw a hand impression clear as day.

"Excuse me. Has anyone collected this?" With the point of a pen she showed them, but just like she was very professional about her job, so was most of the case agents on the team.

"Yes, ma'am. One of the first things we saw," an agent answered.

"Good, 'cause that's clear as day," Trish shot back and continued to look around for anything missed. This case was very important and she wanted to be as helpful as possible. After twenty minutes of looking and coming up with nothing she made her way back up to finish the interview with the funeral director.

He was seated in his chair behind his desk. He had a cup of coffee sitting in front of him while reading over some paperwork. He looked up from the paper when Trish approached. "Here is a paper the woman began to fill out but stopped. I forgot to give it to the other people who interviewed me." The director gave her the paper across the table. It was a first and last name and two numbers to an address on the paper.

Trish was careful not to touch anything but the tiny corner of the paper in order to preserve evidence. It could be prints all over it. There was no telling. She placed the paper in a plastic bag and asked, "May I have a seat?"

"Yes, ma'am," the director said and waved her to any chair.

"So, tell me this. How did this woman look?" Trish asked. She took out a pen and paper to write notes.

"Oh, she's a beauty." The conversation lasted thirty minutes. He told her exactly what happened, what time and what he did. He was very cooperative and gave a detailed description of the woman.

By the time the conversation was over, Trish had gotten another call. It was from the video techs. "Williams speaking."

"We have a video image of an unidentified person, but it doesn't show him approach the van. It's from a far off distant, and video enhance was done, to no avail."

"Okay. I'll come in and take a look."

"Yes, ma'am," the agent said.

Trish was disappointed with the news, but just seeing a subject on tape was better than nothing at all. She hung up her cell to refocus on the interview. "Well, sir, thank you for your kind cooperation. If you remember anything or see anything then give us a call, okay?" Trish said to the funeral director.

Brad

Brad and another case agent were out on stake at Icey and Pimp's home. Nobody was there but activity on the streets was still heavy due to an unrelated crime. Brad knew he could not blend in right now on the block, so they rode through and kept going.

"Let's grab a bite to eat and hopefully we can spot them in the streets. You know they're new to the city. They just might be sight-seeing," Brad told the case agent who drove the unmarked car.

"Good idea," the agent said back.

They rode past, hidden behind dark tints, and after a few turns they found the busy streets of Buckhead. Brad wanted something quick so they chose Mr. Moe's Barbeque Joint that was famous for the sauce.

"Man, I hope this stuff good," the agent made small talk. He was another white dude. He was older and been in the agency longer than Brad. He was from Georgia and worked law enforcement his entire adult life. "Ever since Mr. Moe's been dead, it seems as though the food don't taste good at all."

"Don't say that," Brad replied. He didn't want to spend his money on food that wasn't going to be good.

"Don't get me wrong, the food good. It's just Mr. Moe was like family to me," the agent said and pulled into the restaurant.

Inside the place it was beautifully decorated and had a very warm feeling to it. The food smelled so good that it made them even more hungry as they took seats close by the window to survey the streets.

Within moments a waiter approached to take their orders. Brad had ribs and rolls while the agent went soul food. Both had water to drink. The waiter left with a to do list.

"So, let me ask you your personal opinion," the agent spoke once the waiter left.

"I'm listening."

"Do you think one man is capable of such an act? Or do you think it's an organization of some sort?"

"No, I think it's one man." Brad was being blunt. He was almost certain that the guy on the video was Pimp. He just had to prove it.

"That's crazy. I just wonder sometimes, what's going through some of these folks' minds?" the agent stated and looked out to the traffic.

Brad kindly agreed with a nod of his own head because the agent was right about what he said. Brad too wondered why people did things they've done. Especially Pimp. Like where did he get his mind from and how could someone be so cruel? One day soon Brad knew he would find out the truth. "Me too."

The food shortly arrived and neither agent wasted time eating their hot meals. It took them no longer than five minutes to knock the plates off. They were back in the car, back in traffic within minutes.

Brad was looking into traffic when he saw Icey and Pimp sitting at the light on the left side of them. Both were looking straight ahead, and if any time they would turn and look, they would have seen Brad in the next car over. The light changed and they pulled off.

"Follow them." Brad quickly told his partner what was going on so that he could be on the same page. "Those are the two suspects there in that Benz truck." Brad pointed. He had made the decision not tell anyone about him and Icey being best friends. He'd leave that in Miami because the first time he almost messed up.

The agent was only three cars behind when he saw who Brad pointed at. He made the car slow down so that he could get a little more space between them, just in case Pimp was watching his surroundings. He didn't want them to be spotted by him.

"I guess getting a bite to eat is out the question, huh?" the agent asked.

"I'm hoping they make a quick stop." Brad laughed at the joke but he was serious.

"Don't look like it," the agent shot back when he noticed Pimp turn off the main street that was coming up on his right side. He had to make a quick decision to either turn and follow or keep going.

He kept going because Brad said, "Keep going. I know where he's going."

All the other agent did was keep going until Brad directed him to make a turn which was two streets down. He made the turn and kept driving.

"Slow it down and make this left," Brad continued to direct. The car made the turn just in time to see the tail end of Pimp's ride pulling into his driveway.

"What now?"

"Pull over right here," Brad spoke as he tried to get focused on the house. He could slightly see through the bush but he did get a glimpse of both Icey and Pimp.

"Don't forget we haven't ate," the agent had to remind Brad. *They weren't ready for a stake out right now, no way*, he thought.

"Yeah, my stomach won't let me forget," replied Brad and began to get comfortable.

Jerry Jackson

Chapter 21
Gangsta

"Who the fuck is that nigga?" Montay asked out loud to anyone who had the answer. Everyone was at Gangsta's loft in downtown Atlanta, watching the tape over and over again.

On the surveillance tape, you could see the security guard leave the crib, but didn't fix the alarm to activate it when he left. It showed the two dudes enter the crib ten minutes exactly after security left, which to everyone looked like an inside job.

"Who is that?" Kash asked the security guy who was duct taped to a chair and chained down. He had been beaten already and was barely breathing. Kash lifted his face up so he could see the TV screen. The security guy's face was busted badly. "Who is this nigga!"

"I swear, man, I don't know! I'll never cross y'all, my nigga, for real," he spoke through a bloody mouth.

"Mekka on her way over. She can tell us, I bet," Montay said.

"Man, this bitch right here gonna tell us," Meco said he walked across the room and slapped the security guard so hard with the gun that it knocked him out cold.

"Ease up, Don." Gangsta gave orders to chill and Meco did.

Two Shooters woke the security up and picked the chair upright.

"Man, Gangsta, I swear my nigga—"

"Bro, I don't care to hear that. I want some answers about my friend." Gangsta cut him off quickly.

"Duct tape that nigga mouth," Kash demanded. "Mekka will be here in a minute."

The security dude's mouth instantly got taped up, regardless of his cries and head shaking. Gangsta continue to watch the murder take place. His heart was heavy as he watched his partner fight for his life on his birthday. Gangsta wanted so badly to find out who the other nigga was that got away because police didn't give the info of the dead to anyone yet, and he was hoping Mekka had it when she arrived.

Montay was happy to know the killer wasn't Pimp because going to war with him would be hard and long. He was happy that someone he was cool with didn't cross his team, but he was saddened by looking at the murder take place. It crushed Montay to watch Monkey get killed; to see him get shot in the back of his head and still tried to put up a fight.

"Somebody know what's going on. Boy, when I find out, a nigga ass dead, I swear." Kash wanted to choke someone badly. You could see it in his face. He just hated the thought that a nigga tried the cartel in any type of way, form or fashion. People knew who the crew was so why did they play with fire when they knew it would burn?

Kash wasn't as close to Monkey as Gangsta was, but he had grown to like Monkey and respected his grind. Everyone was like family and the love was real, so when the streets took Monkey it took a good nigga, and someone had to pay for it and fast.

Loco and his crew hadn't said a thing. They just sat around and waited for the go 'head to handle whatever business that needed to be handled. Gangsta was the one that was truly messed up about it. He was just trying to handle everything with the team and remain strong.

Another twenty minutes had gone by that seemed like an hour or two. Mekka had pulled up just in time because the cartel wanted answers and they wanted them now.

Kash spotted her when she pulled up and told the crew. "Mekka just pulled up."

That statement brought life to everyone. Gangsta went to the door to meet her. The security guard also gained a little life because he knew he would be put in the clear, or least that's what he thought.

Mekka was looking tired of crying, restless and heartbroken. She looked like she would fall out at any moment. Gangsta met her in the hallway and embraced her with a warm hug.

She hugged him tight and broke down crying badly. "I don't know what to do, Gangsta. They took my rock," she stated.

"I know, baby girl. We gonna figure this shit out. I swear we are," Gangsta told her.

They walked into the loft. Kash walked over and gave her a hug. Gangsta shut the door.

"The dude who died with Monkey was like an uncle to us. He's my uncle's best friend, who's been around us our whole life," Mekka said

"Hold up, hold up." Kash walked over to the TV screen and pointed. "So, who is this?" He pointed to the dude that got away.

"That resembles my uncle."

"I think I saw this one at the club," Montay added and pointed to the dead one.

"Yeah, he was there last night. My uncle and some more of my family," said Mekka.

"So, you think that's your uncle?" Gangsta asked because to him it didn't matter which family member it was, they were going to die for the actions they took on Monkey.

"Yes. To me it looks like it could be him. He has the same build and height. It's no coincidence that his best friend is dead in my brother's house, ya' know."

"You right," Kash agreed

Gangsta turned to Loco and nodded. Loco turned to his men and spoke Spanish to them. Gangsta had plans to personally murder Monkey's uncle because that was fucked up on his part to even consider crossing his own nephew. Loco was sending his men out to kidnap Monkey's uncle and bring him back to Gangsta.

"What the fuck was he thinking?" Meco finally opened his mouth after just sitting there through everything everyone said.

"He's just a greedy sonofabitch. Monkey had cut him off and he just hateful as fuck. I can't stand his ass," Mekka said.

"Yeah, me either," Gangsta had to add because now he saw the clear picture of what happened.

Mekka stayed over for another hour talking to Kash and Gangsta. Then, she decided she would leave. Gangsta walked her out.

"Thank you so much, G." She hugged him at her car.

"Man, we family. I'll always be there for you, Mekka, and I'ma hold Monkey's kids down. I promise," Gangsta replied. Simultaneously, he saw two cars and a Sprinter van pull into the parking lot.

From his experience, when people rolled like that, it's either one or two things about to happen. It was the police or the jack boys.

Mekka got in her car. Gangsta closed the door for her while watching the van park and the two cars kept going around to another section of the loft.

She rolled the window down and said, "I'll call you tomorrow morning, G."

"Yeah. Do that," he shot back. He took a step back and looked over to the van that nobody got out of. He eased up the walkway toward his loft. Who was in the van? What were they up to? He wasn't really worried about the police because everyone in his loft was straight. Wasn't nothing criminal going on just yet, so what was the issue?

When Gangsta entered the loft, his phone started ringing. It was Loco so he picked up. "Wassup?"

"We got 'em. We back. Do we need to bring him in?"

"Nawl. I have a location for him. Where you at with 'em?"

"I'm in the parking lot. Black van." So, it was Loco in the Sprinter.

"Okay. We coming out now."

Everyone who was loaded up in the house prepared to leave. This was the moment the entire squad was waiting for. It was finally that time.

Chapter 22
Trish

The palm print found at the funeral home produced no leads, no suspect. This news discouraged Trish but didn't make her fold. She also looked at the tape from the store behind the funeral home and all there was to see was an image of a slim, light skinned guy but he didn't get in the van.

The unidentified woman was likely hard to find as well because all they had was a half filled out form and a description of her. Trish would not give up and she trusted the process of how things went.

She continued to go through paperwork, reading everything. She did not want to miss a beat and that's when it hit her. That's when she realized she slipped. Trish quickly got up from her desk, and grabbed her gun, badge and cell phone. She needed to get back across town while it was still early.

The case was still fresh and she vowed to bring the criminal to justice, especially after hearing more than 100 people were killed in the bombing. It was heavy on her heart knowing this happened to innocent people. It could have been her on duty and was killed. Then what? She could not imagine leaving her husband and family. Trish shook her head at the thought and walked out her office. FBI officials were coming and going as she passed, headed to the elevator.

One of the case agents approached her. "Mrs. Williams, I think I have something good. Do you have a moment's time?" the agent asked.

"Depends on how good it is," she replied.

"Okay. It's witnesses who saw the guy who murdered the senator's daughter and boyfriend. And hear this. He's light skinned and about the same build as the guy behind the funeral home on the camera."

"Really?" She was surprised.

"Yes."

"Well, I tell you what. Hold this info until I get back or you can ride with me and brief me on everything," Trish offered.

"I have no problem with that."

With that said, they waited for the elevator. Trish was extra happy for that news. It could be a connection there with the shooter and bomber. She surely hoped so.

She was hopeful that it was some form of surveillance tape of the woman who entered the funeral home at one of the many stores that lined the busy streets. The elevator door opened and the two agents stepped on, both determine to solve this case.

Again, Veedoo crossed her mind. She was missing her husband so she decided to text him and tell him he was on her mind. All she wanted right now was to be under him, kiss on him and be held by him. All she wanted was her Veedoo.

Gangsta

Everyone walked to the parking lot of the loft, leaving onlookers to watch them. It was at least 15 people. Everyone got into their cars and trucks. Gangsta and Kash went to the van. Kash knocked on the side of the van and moments later it slid open. There they saw a guy bound by hands and feet. His mouth was covered with duct tape. They could tell he had been in a small struggle due to spots of blood on his shirt and swelling over his eye.

Kash and Gangsta climbed in and closed the sliding door to the van.

"So, this the pussy nigga?" Kash asked while pushing the uncle's face back to get a good look at him.

"Nigga, what's your problem?" Gangsta asked as the van had pulled off. He snatched the tape from the uncle's mouth.

"Man, I'm telling y'all I'd never do my family like that!" He was crying.

Kash laughed. "Shut the fuck up, big ass nigga. Yo' ass was so gangsta when you ran up in our shit."

"Man, I swear—"

"Fuck all that! Just tell us this and you will get spared. Did the security guard help y'all niggas?" Gangsta wanted to know.

The uncle was hesitant first. He looked from Kash to Gangsta. He tried desperately to read between the lines because he wanted his life spared. "It was his idea," he lied.

"The security?" Kash asked, surprised at how quick he flipped on his help.

"Yeah, man. I'm sorry. That was my nephew—"

"Fuck nigga, shut up." Gangsta walked over to the uncle and straddled his lap. With one motion, he snapped his neck.

When he stood up, Loco and Kash just looked at him but said nothing. It'd been years since Gangsta had taken a life, and that was apart of him that he kept tucked away so it surprised his two friends when he just blacked out like he did.

"Get this pussy nigga out of here." Gangsta kicked the dead uncle in his face, snapping his already broken neck once more. He was mad and they could see it on his face.

Loco, on the other hand, was thinking when he said, "That's not a good idea. Let's take him to a secluded area and bury him there, 'cause if we pull a dead body out of this van, we will have some explaining to do."

It didn't take Gangsta but one minute to realize that Loco was right about which action to take. Kash even agreed with a nod.

"You right. Just let me out." Gangsta pushed passed Kash and open the sliding door. He was mad. He turned around and said, "Bring me that nigga's eyes when y'all done." Then, he walked off.

Kash, on the other hand, looked at the dead body and smiled. This was right up his alley. He rubbed his hands together. He was ready to get to it.

Jerry Jackson

Chapter 23
Pimp

Pimp called Montay but got no answer, so he put his phone down on his night stand and found his girl in the bathroom. She was getting dressed and doing her hair a different way than it was today. He walked up behind her. "And where are you going?" He kissed her cheek.

"I'm about to go Atlanta shopping— get my nails and feet done then come home and cook you a dinner that you better be home to eat." Icey slightly turned around.

They quickly kissed. He then stood on the side of her. "So how long you plan on being gone, baby, 'cause I got to make a quick run on business," Pimp stated.

"Just a few hours. No more than three, baby, but I want you home before I get home," she shot back.

"I got cha." Pimp smiled and walked out of the bathroom. He had plans of his own today and didn't know how he would break away from Icey, but she just gave him the go 'head.

Checking his phone, he read the message Honey sent earlier. She wanted to see him today. He, on the other hand, wanted to know what was up with Montay and his urgent calls. Pimp was just hoping it wasn't serious enough to get his attention and keep it.

When he walked outside, the sky was a pretty bright blue, the sun was shining hard and the clouds were as white as snow. The air moved just enough to give his skin a little tingle. Something didn't feel right to Pimp as he looked over his front yard, then side to side. Upon surveying, he thought he saw through some bushes that separated his yard. He thought he saw a car sitting there. Pimp got into his ride. He decided to act oblivious just to see what was going on. *Maybe it was the police still at the home next door*, he thought and crank up the ride.

When he pulled out of his driveway a moment later, the car was gone. He pulled over to the exact spot he thought he saw the car parked. He got out and looked around in the streets and what he saw shocked him. Pimp could not believe it was a napkin from a local coffee shop that someone had written on. It was clear that the FBI was doing surveillance on him for a two-week period, six hours each day, starting today. Pimp could only shake his head because the feds seemed to never stop.

He got back into the ride now knowing he was being followed by the feds, so he would act accordingly. What did they possibly want now? He was pretty sure it was about the shit that happened in Miami, and right now he didn't have the time to be dealing with these folks about that situation.

As he rode through the Buckhead area, he acted oblivious to the tail behind him five cars back that he finally spotted.

"So, y'all bitches wanna play, huh?" Pimp asked himself as he carefully watched them follow him.

One quick turn down a side street Pimp pulled into the first driveway he saw, and just as quick got out the car. He knew it would take at least one minute for the tail to turn on the same street so he stood there on the side walk, holding the napkin in his hand. Pimp knew the rules and regulations and knew if surveillance was spotted then they would stop following him. One thing about the FBI was that they were very professional. So, to slip, they wouldn't like it.

Just as he had predicted, the car turned on the street. Pimp made sure to stand out, holding the napkin up facing them. When the car passed by, Pimp had got the shock of his life when he made direct eye contact with Brad. Even though he was taken aback by seeing Brad, he didn't give off the surprised look. He continued to hold up the napkin until they passed.

The agents kept driving while Pimp turned in their direction, still holding the napkin up in his hand until the car disappeared around the corner.

"Punk bitch."

Now Pimp knew they were on to him and were trying to build a case against him or his entire operation. Brad was a dead man walking because he just didn't get it. The only true reason he was still living was because of Icey, and Pimp didn't want to see her hurt. Now Pimp didn't give two shits about the relationship between them. Brad was in his business and had plenty of potential to mess things up.

He got back into his ride, pulled out of the driveway and decided that he would see if he could catch up with them and tail them back. Pimp pressed the gas to the floor. The car sped down the residential street in search of the FBI, but he didn't see the car and came up to a stop sign.

His phone started ringing as he made a right turn onto the main street. He picked up. "Yeah?"

"What's up with you, my guy?" It was Montay.

"Shit, bro. Wassup wit it?" asked Pimp and turned on another street.

"Can you meet me? I need to rap wit cha," Montay shot back.

"Yeah, we can link. I'm still in the Buckhead area. Where are you?"

"I'm at my crib. Just pull up. I'm waiting on ya'."

"Cool. I'll be there, bro," Pimp replied and they hung up the call. He couldn't help but wonder what Montay wanted. He damn sure hoped it wasn't dealing with drugs and anything illegal. He had enough stuff on his plate right now to take on anything else. Plus, the FBI was in town again and this too was another obstacle to climb over.

If it wasn't one thing, it was another. It's always something in the way of his elevation, of his success, either wrong or right, and Pimp was truly sick of it. He knew he could not just quit and give up his journey, but at times he just wanted a break from everything. His mind and body needed rest, but he wouldn't stop. Within minutes Pimp found the highway. He got on and instantly got in a tunnel vision.

Jerry Jackson

Chapter 24
Trish

The evidence was building on Pimp and his connection to the bombing. Now it was two witnesses who pointed out Pimp in a six-picture line up, saying he was the shooter of the senator's daughter and her boyfriend. These statements were good but not good enough for an arrest to be made. They needed more evidence that it was Savarous in the parking lot.

Trish had agents all over Atlanta going to every van rental place and found that nobody rented a van fitting the description of Pimp. Trish didn't stop there though, and dug deeper and found out that two days before the bombing an unidentified woman rented a van for three days and reported the van stolen. This was a good lead and instantly Trish and a team of agents descended upon the rental place.

"Special agent Williams," she said to the woman behind the deck and flashed her ID.

The woman looked at the ID and politely spoke back. "How are you, ma'am? May I help you?"

"Yes, I'd like you to look at some photos and answer a few questions." Trish pulled the picture of Pimp out and passed it across the counter toward the lady. "Have you seen this man?"

The woman looked at the picture a moment's time. "No, ma'am. I can't say that I have," the woman said and gave Trish the picture back.

"Can you pull all recent rental files? I see you have surveillance. Can you also replay events dated a few days back?"

"Yes. I can get the things you need, just give me a moment," the young woman said and left the front desk. She returned shortly with a bind of paperwork. She also had with her a disc.

"Question. A van reported stolen from here, did it ever turn up?" Trish wanted to see the kind of answer she would get.

"No, ma'am. It's with the police, I guess," the woman replied and started looking for something. She was going through some paperwork and finally found what she was looking for. "This is the background check on the woman who rented the van and reported it stolen."

When Trish saw the paper she instantly saw the comparison in hand writing. It was a different name and address. "Thank you. If you, by any chance, find anything else please give me a call," said Trish, giving her a card then hand shake.

She and the team went back to the office with these new findings, happy that things were looking better and better. It was a team also out where the daughter was murdered, asking questions to any and everyone. Trish was excited to know what was going on and connecting the dots was fun. It was and seemed as easy as chewing bubblegum.

Again, her husband crossed her mind as she rode back to the office. She decided to go ahead and text him again just to let him know she was thinking so much about him, about them and everything they shared. She loved their love and was happy with the life they lived.

Veedoo texted back just as she expected. He was the type of man that was home when she got there. He was that man that handled business and made sure home was secure. What more could a girl ask for? Her train of thought was interrupted by one of the case agents asking her a question.

"Mrs. Williams, giving the evidence thus far, how long should it take to make an arrest?" The young case agent asked.

Her phone began to ring while she was thinking about the question. She looked and saw it was another agent. Trish put her hand up, telling him to give her a moment, then she answered. "Yes, agent?"

"Ma'am, our surveillance was blown. The perp saw us, and not only does he know we're following him, he somehow got our schedule."

"Schedule? How so, sir?" Trish was shocked by this news.

"My partner was writing notes and somehow it fell out of the window," the other agent told her.

"Goodness. Okay, place a hold on doing a stake. We need to get close to him though. Just meet us at the office, agent, so I can brief everyone."

"Yes, ma'am. I'll be there," Brad said and they disconnected.

This news wasn't good at all. She didn't want the suspect to get scared and try to leave the state. It's always better when you could survey a suspect without them knowing what's going on. It makes the case better and the FBI was very, very slick about how they did things.

It took another twenty minutes to get to the office. On the way over, Trish took that time to answer the young agent's question. She could tell he would someday make a good FBI commander if he remained as eager as he was to learn things. Trish could remember when she begun, how she wanted to know everything and anything that she didn't understand. She found somebody that could help her understand it. It's what made her the agent she was today. For that drive, she was thankful. Trish knew she had another 20 years of this field work, and by then she should be very high in the agency. She planned to retire from the FBI and live happily ever after with Veedoo, have one or two more kids and just sailing through life is her direct plan. She knew Veedoo was already out the game, so twenty years from now, he should be as clean as a whistle from any and everything. *He just needed to continue the journey he was walking and do not change up*, she thought.

Pimp

Montay's wife was away with the kids so nobody was there when Pimp pulled up to the house. Montay's shooter was on the porch when Pimp got out his whip. He was pretty sure he had lost the tail that was on him, and even more certain that they would try and switch up their offense.

"What's good? Montay expecting me," Pimp told the armed shooter who was clearly carrying an A-K 47. Pimp wasn't feeling it but couldn't say anything about how they operated.

"Yeah. He in there waiting on you." The shooter nodded toward the door that Pimp was supposed to go through.

Pimp walked into the crib to find Montay at the pool table. A pool table that was full of stacks of Money. He also had boxes of what looked like cocaine sitting by the pool table.

He looked up and saw Pimp walk in. He smiled. "What's up, bro? I need cha."

Pimp didn't take his eyes off the dope. "Talk to me."

"Come sit with me, brother." Montay walked over to the sofa.

Pimp followed where they took seats.

"I'm trying to get out the game, bro." Montay paused again, trying to collect his thoughts. He did not want to say the wrong things because he needed Pimp's help. "I got to move this work and clean this money and I know you know what you're doing. I know and understand that you trying to lay low and shit, but I'm stuck, bro. This was Monkey's shit."

Pimp couldn't do nothing but just look at him for a minute. He had too much going on to be jumping into the game, especially since he saw that the feds were back up to their bullshit. "Shit, bro, my mind ain't nowhere near that dope shit. I got to think about my shit first. I got to get my shit together first. Feel me?" Pimp didn't know what else to say but he had to keep it real with his boy before lying.

"I know, bro, and I can't be mad at you for that. Gangsta and Kash got me working hard, man, and I'm trying to get out the game. ain't shit in it once you have made a million or two. The next places are the chain gang or the graveyard, and I don't want either."

"That's what I'm talking about," Pimp added. "Don't them niggas know you want out?"

Montay didn't answer right away. He sat there with a thoughtful look upon his face, then he finally spoke. "Not really. I'm not gonna even lie, my nigga. It's like I don't know how to tell bro I want out when he the reason I'm up. I know the situation and I'm a factor in this family, so it's hard to just drop it ya', feel me?" Montay was stressing.

"So, what exactly you got to do with all this shit?" Pimp asked, getting up to walk closer to the dope.

"I got to drop the dope off to my man's, but it's the money what I'm talking about. It's like nine- million in cash."

Usually Pimp would take a nigga off for that amount of money on hand. He was drained and he was hot. He didn't think he would want to fuck with the cartel either, because they had a mean set up. Pimp gave it some deep thought for a moment. He really didn't have the right tools or contacts to be touching that type of money. Montay was from Atlanta, so why was it so hard for him to get the help? However it went, Pimp could only do what he was able to do. With that, he said, "Bro, the only help I can give you is I can hide that paper for a smooth year, but that's it. I don't know what else to tell you, bro."

"A year? I need the money clean, bro. I'm talking about going back to Miami with me for a few months—" Montay couldn't even finish his statement when Pimp stopped him.

"That's never gonna happen. I got a baby on the way, my nigga, I'm super hot down there. Ain't no way you asking me that." Pimp was clearly pissed.

"Nawl, bro, don't think like that. I'm just saying I know you have the source down there and we just doing clubs. No drugs, my nigga. We just cleaning the money, that's it. Just having fun. It shouldn't take but two months tops. I was thinking your baby mother has the school down there, so you—"

He was cut off once again by Pimp. "Bro, you dead. You can kill that Miami, shit my nigga. I told you what I will do. It's nothing on that shit, fool." Pimp gave him that look which every street nigga had when it's no more talking.

Montay was far from soft but it was a mutual respect of the codes that made him leave the issue alone. "My bad, bro. You know my intentions are not to get you fucked up. I'm just stressing. That's it. I understand fully what you saying, bro." Montay gave him some dap and a shoulder to shoulder hug. "You ate? Let's grab something to eat," he suggested.

"I got a meal waiting on me, my nigga, but we can slide to the game tomorrow if possible. I'm about to get my ass home," Pimp told him. He still had to pull up on Honey before making it to dinner.

He would not and could not disrespect his wife and their first dinner at home.

"I feel that. I just know my wife not gonna even be home. I just wanted to kick it. Shid, I might as well suit up in the Timb's and hit the block." Montay kind of laughed at his own statement.

They slapped five once again and Pimp left. He had other business to handle.

Chapter 25
Honey

Honey was still as sexy as ever. Pimp noticed when she opened the door wearing a lemonade colored crop top and a pair of fitting sweats with no socks. Pimp approved with a nod. He stepped in as she closed the door behind him. Her scent was smelling good.

"So, how you like this spot?" He asked walking around, looking to make sure they were alone.

"It's okay, I guess," Honey replied as she went into the kitchen.

He came from behind. "We'll upgrade you in a few months. I know you ready for your lil' girl, huh?" Pimp asked while gripping her bubble booty.

She continued to do what she was doing and answered, "Yes. I can't wait."

"I got cha. So, listen. I told you that I owe you the world. You always been down with a nigga and I won't trust nobody else." Pimp was leaning on the countertop. "I need you to run my grocery store which means you got to be trained for this position."

When he finished his statement, Honey turned around to face him with a certain look. "I'm saying, does this mean I got to put my daughter off?"

"Hell no. Good thing about this is you get in-home training, and I'm not saying just right now, baby girl because it's still being built. But in the next year, we will be in full swing." Pimp tried to explain as best as he could.

"Well, that's fine with me, baby."

"That's what's up. That's why I love you, girl."

"You sure haven't been giving me the dick. Wifey must got you drained?" She jokingly asked but Pimp knew she was serious. She was about to turn back to the sink, but when Pimp advanced toward her she stopped.

"We both been busy, baby. You know what's up." He had his hand on her pussy, applying pressure while looking in her eyes. Honey's pussy was fat and juicy as he rotated his hand through the pressure.

"Don't start," she said and pushed his hand. She turned back to the sink to finish the dishes.

"Put this shit down." Pimp reached around her, taking the glass out her hand. He took her by the wrist, pulling her out the kitchen.

Honey didn't put up a fight. She just went with the flow. In the living room, Pimp made her take a seat on her sofa. He stood there in front of her and started to unbuckle his belt, still looking her in the eyes. He moved in a slow manner but had managed to get his pants open and his dick out.

Honey took him in her hand. She wrapped her fingers around his hardness. She had been missing it and him so much. Honey got comfortable. She leaned her head to the side and with one motion she licked up and down his length. When she came up the second time, she took just his head in her warm mouth with quick circles of her tongue.

Pimp held her head in place and began to grind into her mouth, making his dick slide in deeper. She still had skills. He could tell because she didn't fight him off and gave him good throat. Honey held onto him as he fucked her face.

"Yeah, baby, that's what I'm talking about," Pimp said through a moan. He took his dick out her mouth, holding his dick and her chin. He bounced his dick up and down across her lips. He slipped it back in.

Honey grabbed the base of his dick and started sucking and slurping him fast, twisting her head.

It had him on his toes, now holding her neck, loving the feeling she delivered.

"C'mere." Pimp pulled away a second time.

She was sucking the dick so good that he had to fuck her one time real quick. She stood up and Pimp pulled her sweats down. She stepped out of them along with her panties. Still fine as ever, still sexy as hell, Pimp admired her physique, then stood up.

He turned her to face the couch and made her bend at the waist. Honey's pussy was already wet from just sucking his dick so it was easy to slide inside her walls. Honey moaned loud as he entered.

"Ahhh, shit, bae." She gripped the sofa back as Pimp held her hips, pulling her down to his thrust of warm, hard dick. "Ummh. Mmh. Pimp."

"Don't run. C'mere. Let me up in this pussy," Pimp said and went deeper.

"Shit!"

"Arch that back," Pimp encouraged.

She did as she was told and put an arch in her back. Pimp started beating the pussy real good.

"Dang, bae, this dick so good. Lord, bae, give it to me. This pussy is yours, I swear." Honey moaned loud. She buried her face in the sofa's back that was still gripped in her hands.

"This pussy so good," Pimp spoke while long-stroking her. He had one feet on the sofa seat and one on the floor, doing his thang.

"Baby. Bae. I'm finna nut. Oh, this pussy is 'bout to nut, daddy. Oh, don't stop! Don't stop! Ohhh, please! Yes, just like that, bae. Don't stop. Don't stop. Ohh, I'm cuming, baby! I'm cuming! Bae, I'm. Ohhh! Arghh!" Honey moaned and grunted as her orgasm crashed through her

It was a mission completed for Pimp. All he wanted was her satisfied and he handled that business properly. Pimp didn't hang around long after the quick session because Icey was at home and waiting on him. He had promised to make it to their first meal together in their new home. Pimp cleaned himself up in her bathroom and left her spot. He walked out of her apartment not knowing FBI agents were staking out and had already taken photos and video as he made it to his ride.

Jerry Jackson

Chapter 26
Trish

Her name was Lisa McCants. She was from North Carolina, born and raised, with a daughter. Trish stared at the picture of this pretty woman. She looked young and full of life and Trish wasn't surprised to see that she didn't have a record.

At the office, Trish was able to compare notes with other agents about everything and she quickly made connections between Pimp and Lisa, AKA Honey. They had enough to make an arrest, but it wasn't enough to get a conviction. It was not enough evidence pointing toward Pimp. So, the FBI had put together a scenario of what took place. Pimp had killed the senator's daughter and boyfriend. He had Lisa rent the van and then report it stolen. Pimp then proceeded to the funeral home. Lisa entered the front while Pimp broke in through the back and placed the bombs.

As crazy as it seemed, it's the best logical answer to everyone's questions. Trish wanted to be positive with their approach so she had 24-hour surveillance on Honey, and within the first hour of survey she had gotten a call from one of the field agents saying that Pimp was leaving Honey's apartment. Trish couldn't believe the instant news. It was good and it was a bigger leap in the case. Now all she had to do was figure out how to get surveillance on Pimp without him knowing. He already knew the feds were lurking around him so they had to get around this.

"Special agent Williams, what if we slip listening devices in his girl's car and gamble on the hope that one day he gets in and hold a conversation?" One of the agents asked. Everyone was working tirelessly to break this case.

"See if it's possible to pull it off," Trish shot back.

"Results have come back from the lab about the dirt and bomb material," another agent spoke.

"Okay?"

"It's negative from caparison of the bomb material from the funeral," the agent hated to say.

It was the news she wasn't looking for but it didn't hurt the case. They had too much circumstantial evidence on Pimp and Honey. Trish just needed to put it together properly. "Okay, and who's the agent that's surveying Jones?" Trish asked. It was a room full of agents, all who were working on the case. She was looking around until she saw a hand held in the air.

"Special agent responsible is me, ma'am."

"Your name, agent?"

"Special agent Smith," the white man said. He was your average white dude with a skinny build and long brown hair. He was younger than most agents. Trish could tell instantly.

"And your senior, sir?" Trish asked and that's when another agent spoke up.

"Special agent Brad Jennie, ma'am." This agent she could tell was seasoned. He was one of the agents that helped most with this case.

Both agents knew they were in trouble and would get a single meeting with Trish's senior. Right now, she just informed them that they needed to report to her office. She wasn't into embarrassing people.

"I'll see both you in my office after the meeting," she said and received nods from both guys as expected.

They jumped right into the case again.

"Brad, I need you to also be a teacher. I want you to hit the ground running against and see if we can find another witness. Find anything that could be used to help this case," Trish said to him and his partner. Then, she turned to the other agents. "Everyone else, continue to work as you were. Good job, everyone, for being fast on your feet. Now, let's work."

She ended the meeting so people could go home, get showers and hit the streets again. She couldn't wait to get these statements from the two agents so that she could make it home herself. She was missing Veedo so badly that she could practically smell his scent.

Once the meeting room was cleared, Trish made it to her office. Moments later, the agents were knocking at her door. She looked up from reading her computer screen and waved them in.

Brad was older and bigger than the new agent Smith.

Trish pointed out the forms they needed to write statements. "Now, you both know that this is something serious. Especially you, Brad. What were you thinking? What were you doing? You couldn't have been doing your jobs as the detail required. I need statements from both of you, and please make it fast."

Brad grabbed the forms and pens, handing his partner one of each. Then, they took their seats.

Trish looked at them as if they had lost their minds. "Excuse me. Go into your comfort zones for this, but hurry up. I'm leaving shortly."

Brad seemed as if he was about to say something about Trish being so demanding and so direct, but he thought against it. He and his partner stood.

"Yes, ma'am. Give me a minute," Smith said as he followed Brad, who didn't say anything, out of the door.

Hell, she didn't care about his or anyone else's attitude. I was, and forever would be, all business and nothing personal. She always did her job. She started cleaning up, preparing to leave so she could get to her soulmate. Work was work, but home was different.

After another ten minutes, the agents returned, handing over their statements and pens. Trish took them and locked up her office. It was time to go home.

"Okay! I'll see everyone in a few hours! I'm on call if anything changes or takes place that demands my attention," Trish spoke to the entire office.

Everyone agreed with her before they all left.

Jerry Jackson

Chapter 27
Gangsta

The very next morning when Gangsta opened his eyes, his heart was heavy with sorry over his friend being killed. To make matters worse, he was setup by someone who was paid to protect them. Gangsta hated sour niggas and disloyal bitches. He sat up in the bed and could hear the faint sounds of music. It was either his daughter or Junior, because Ne-Ne had a doctor's appointment. They were expecting their second child together.

He got up and grabbed his phone. Then, he sent out a group text that only said, *"Urgent issues."*

It was understood that when and if this code was sent out by Loco, Kash and Gangsta, it meant that everyone in the cartel had to be there for the meeting. The location and time was already understood of where the meeting would take place. Gangsta called the gathering because he needed everyone on the same page.

After sending the text, he into the bathroom to get fresh. He jumped in the shower and cleaned himself up. Just as quickly, he was dressed in a pair of jeans and a white t-shirt. The only thing he left the house with was his cellphone. Before leaving, he saw his daughter walking around, talking on her phone. Junior was playing the game with music blasting. Gangsta didn't even bother them. Instead, he continued out the door.

He had security 24/7 and a heavily guarded secret home that only a select few people knew of. Right now, Gangsta didn't know if he could trust the people who worked for him around his family. Monkey being killed had done something to him that he couldn't shake. Gangsta could hardly handle the thought of betrayal. The shit reminded him of Dank's bitch-ass.

"I'm good, Mitch. I'ma slide solo," Gangsta told one of his best drivers.

Mitch had been working for Gangsta since day one. He never displayed any sign of disloyalty, but Gangsta wanted to alone this morning. Mitch nodded and stepped back as Gangsta climbed inside his classic car. It was a baby blue Cutlass 442 with cream guts.

Anytime Gangsta drove this car, it meant that he was headed back to his old ways. Those who knew him knew this. The 442 came to life after two tries, and Gangsta gave it a lot of gas to make the engine holler. He then got out of the Cutlass and went to the trunk of his Benz. He reached inside and pulled out two guns that were on a belt, and a 223 with some clips.

He tossed everything in the trunk of the Cutlass and closed it, then jumped in and pulled out of the driveway. He had to maneuver around Junior's Bentley coupé to get out of his spot. Gangsta had one thing on his mind right now, and later he would go back to being humble. Right now, it was all gas and no brakes.

One thing about this life was that you could be here one day and gone the next. Gangsta also knew how the game went and would forever go when dealing with the streets. It had to be a reaction to every action taken in the streets. You had to either be with it or swift enough to get out of certain situations. Gangsta knew that he had to make this statement for the old and the new. He was already feeling like he let the uncle go out the easy way. He was for sure not going out like this on the security guard who set everything up. Gangsta would not continue to let this pussy ass nigga live like everything was Gucci. Gangsta couldn't do it, no matter if he wanted to or not.

His phone started ringing as he drove through his area. He looked down at the screen and saw that it was Kash calling. He was probably the only person Gangsta would talk to at this moment. He was on a mission and he wasn't missing it at all. "What's hap, foo?" He picked up.

"Bruh, what's the mojo, shawty? What's on your mind, my boy?" Kash knew him well and it showed.

"Everything A-one, foo. Just sliding through the city. Wassup your way?" Gangsta tried to down-play his true emotions.

Kash wasn't having that at all. "I know shit smooth, but what's on my brother's mind? Security?" He had gotten his answer when Gangsta didn't answer him right away. He knew that Gangsta was head out to murder the guard.

"Told you, foo. I'm just rolling through the city this morning. I got da boy Monkey on my mind, bro, but that's 'bout it. I'm smooth though," Gangsta told him.

"Okay, shawty. I was just checking on you. Oh, and I handled that security business this morning for you as well, 'cause I knew you wouldn't get no good rest, my nigga. I was in the area and decided to kill two fuck niggas with the same gun."

That statement had gotten Gangsta's attention. "What's that on, foo?"

"That's on everything we stand on, shawty. You know I don't play games with pussy niggas. I hate 'em." Kash boasted and Gangsta could vouch for it.

"Say less, foo, because I sure was en route. I promise." Gangsta laughed as he drove.

"I know you was. I'm 'bout to lay back with the family until the meeting. I'll rock wit you later. my boy." Kash said.

"Okay, foo. I'll catch you." Gangsta was glad that Kash had called and told him the news of the murdered security guard because Lord knows he didn't want to kill nobody else in life. He just wanted the money so he could take care of his family and friends. That's it, that's all.

Jerry Jackson

Chapter 28
Kash

Kash was sitting in his driveway early. He had just hung up the phone with Gangsta. He knew Gangsta was bothered by Monkey being killed so he had handled the business for his brother. Taking life was just like taking steps to Kash, especially for something good.

He got out his ride. The cool morning air attacked his face. He could smell breakfast being cooked on the inside. Breakfast was what he needed at the moment. Kash reached inside his ride and grabbed a large bag of money. He tossed it over his shoulder and proceeded to the front door.

His daughter, who was a teenager, was coming out of the house followed by both her best friends. "Daddy!" She kissed the side of his face

"Wassup, baby? Hey, ladies," Kash spoke. He was one of the coolest dads ever.

"We headed to tryouts. Wish me luck!"

"And you know it, baby," Kash shot back as she walked to her car.

She was looking just like her mother. He admired that. He went on into the crib— a very large home just for him and his kids. As soon as he entered, his two Pitt-bulls came happily toward him. As vicious as the animals were, when they saw Kash and his kids, they were like puppies.

Kash rubbed both his dogs. He left the bag on the floor and walked toward the kitchen. He was hungry and he had the best cooks in Atlanta cooking for him. His cooks were two older females who Kash had been knowing for years, and they were doing their thing early that morning.

"Ladies, good morning!" Kash spoke as he entered the kitchen. His dogs were well-trained and stopped at the threshold.

"Good morning, Kash. You hungry?" Mrs. Rebecca spoke first.

Then, there was Mrs. Lewis. "I sure hope so. Something told me you were coming home today."

"Most definitely ready to eat." Kash was a different person when he was home. He left all street activity in the streets when he walked through the door. He continued through the kitchen and up some side steps that led to his bedroom.

Inside his master bedroom he began to get undressed so he could get a quick shower before breakfast. Life for Kash the past 12 years had been an amazing journey. Sometimes he wondered how he and Gangsta made it through the shit they had encountered.

Through their journey, they have made many enemies and met some loyal folks, too. Overall, he and Gangsta took care of their families and friends, they made things possible for niggas in the streets and it all came from not folding up in the struggle.

Kash got into the shower. The water was just right and warm when he got under it. It was like his body needed to feel the warmness of the water to relax his mind.

He was a very rich street nigga and he had no plan to stop hustling from state to state. Even if he had to get in the paint himself and slang bricks, he would. But he had a team and many people to feed, so that meant everyone needed to be putting in work like they'd been doing from the beginning, because it was too late to start fumbling.

Pimp

When Pimp made it home, he didn't see anything funny but he knew shit had gotten real and real fast. Feds were following him again and it wasn't good with how he was feeling. His lawyer had told him that the case against him was tossed out and that he was clean in Miami. So, what was this?

He parked the car in his driveway and killed the engine. His big questions about the feds were, "What do they want? What do they have on me?"

Pimp pulled out his phone. He called his lawyer because he didn't have a clue of what was going on and he needed to know. The lawyer's phone rang a couple times before his secretary picked up. Pimp told her the call was urgent. He was quickly placed on a brief hold, then his lawyer jumped on the phone.

"Savarous? How is it going?" The lawyer sounded joyous. His voice was a high-pitch, making Pimp pull the phone away from his ear.

"Everything is all bad from what I see. Why are the feds doing surveillance on me again? I thought this shit was over with," Pimp said to his paid who had to defend any case he's ever had.

"Yes, everything should be good. The conspiracy case is tossed out in Miami. Unless you have done anything in Atlanta, you don't have anything to worry about."

"Okay. So, can you do something about this surveillance shit they got going on?"

"All I can do is see what's going on. Now, I cannot do anything about any new investigation but represent you."

"Well, get on this shit ASAP 'cause the last thing I want is the feds on me in Atlanta."

His lawyer agreed and they ended the call.

Pimp got out the car and walked into his home. Inside the living room was Icey, looking at a morning TV show. She had a small sheet thrown over her as she cuddled with the sofa's pillows. She looked up at her man when he walked in and closed the door behind him.

"What's up, baby?" Pimp walked to her. He leaned down to kiss her.

"Hey, baby."

"What cha doing? How you feeling?" Pimp asked.

"Just looking at this show until ten. I have a doctor's appointment at 11:30. Are you going?"

"Of course, baby. You ate?" Pimp made his way into the kitchen as he talked.

Icey got up from the sofa she followed him. "Yes. Bacon, eggs and toast. Do you want any?"

Pimp turned around to look at her before he asked her, "Did you cook it, baby?"

"I did," Icey proudly replied with her beautiful smile and her stomach protruding out of her shirt, looking as cute as ever.

"Great. Warm it up, baby. I'll be right back." Pimp headed upstairs to quickly wash off any smell of Honey or anything. He wanted to cuddle with his wife this morning for some odd reason. As soon as he walked in the room, however, his phone started ringing. It was his lawyer calling which he instantly picked up. "What's good?"

"Between me and you, it's another case sealed against you. Something recently and big, but I'm not supposed to know this. All I know is that you need to be at my office ASAP so we can talk in person," the lawyer told him.

Pimp's heart dropped. "What do you mean something big?" Pimp hoped it wasn't the bombing.

"This was the message."

"Okay, I'll fly you down." Now, his mind was racing to find a way out of whatever the feds had going on.

He jumped in the shower fast and made it downstairs with Icey. He couldn't show her that he was worried or bothered by something, so he fixed his emotions and ate breakfast with his girl while she sat across from him, telling him of her day alone yesterday. Pimp ate and listened intently to her, but his mind was so overwhelmed with the feds.

One thing that was for certain was that Pimp vowed to get his father's freedom and keep his own in the process. He had no plans on going to prison or anywhere near it. He would not go out like that, no matter what he had to do to stop an indictment.

Chapter 29
Pimp

After breakfast, Pimp and Icey rode together to the doctor's office. He spent his time making all the necessary calls he needed to make. He also booked a private flight for his lawyer to get to Atlanta, Georgia. Pimp called his father's lawyer and told her to speed all process up, dealing with his father.

Icey came from the back of the office.

Pimp put his phone up then hugged his girl. "What's going on with my baby?" he asked. He kissed the side of her face.

"I'm waiting on the doctor. The nurse just took my blood pressure and weight first," Icey replied.

Pimp begin to rub her stomach as he always did at times like this. "I love you, baby."

"I know, baby, and I'm happy you do."

Pimp kissed her stomach. They took seats in the office full of other people who looked on and cheered Pimp on for being so affectionate with his pregnant girl. He bestowed so much respect and love in his actions toward her. He stood up, face to face with her. He looked her in the eyes for a moment while holding both her hands. It was plain and simple to see that Pimp was in love. Icey was captivated by the given fact that he was in love with her. She felt it in everything they shared, especially when he acted like this. He pulled her closer to him until they were nose to nose. He hugged her tight.

"Thank you for this child," he said and released her with a soft kiss on her lips.

"Baby, you are more than welcome." Icey was touched by his actions. Pimp was such a sweetheart when he wanted to be.

Moments later Icey's name was called over the intercom in the office. It was her time to go to the back and see the doctor. Together, hand and hand, they walk to the back, ready for the viewing of their baby. Neither of them realized that it was surveillance on them. Federal agents were also at their house. Neither had any idea how critical this case had become so quickly. Pimp had assumed but he didn't know.

Back in the doctor's office, they learned that Icey was 4 months pregnant and it was a boy. Pimp was extremely happy with the news and it showed in his actions when hearing it. Icey was happy and burst into laughter when she saw how happy Pimp became. It was an amazing site to her. It was priceless.

The doctor took pictures of the baby and gave her a due date. Icey was elated with the news and waiting not a second calling her mother when they left the office. Pimp followed behind her out the door, also on his phone checking his messages.

Feds were taking videos and pictures of them as they approached and got into the car. Pimp's mind was on the message he got from Montay, who wanted to meet Pimp about the help he said he would give. Pimp hit him back and got into the car with Icey. As always, he leaned over and kissed her before cranking up to pull off, and the federal agents even got that.

Gangsta

Loco, Longo and Jeter showed up at Gangsta's doorstep unexpected, but was always welcome there no matter the situation. Gangsta was upstairs with his wife when he was told of his company.

"Everything perfect, baby." Gangsta continued to console Ne-Ne. She was still crying when finding out about Monkey being killed. It crushed her the same as everyone else. It was so sad. "Let me go holla at the team, bae." He kissed the top of his wife's head.

Ne-Ne agreed to let him go to his friends. She tried her best to get right as he got up. He wondered what Loco wanted but knew it was important because he never just popped up like this with Jeter or Longo. Gangsta made it downstairs where the men were waiting in the living room.

Loco stood up to greet him as always. "Way, how are you, my friend?"

"I'm good, way. How are you?"

They shook hands then Loco spoke. "Well, you called an urgent matters meeting. Chavez wants statements of it after its held. Another thing is very important that it's done early as of two hours, starting now. Assemble all parties and record the session."

Gangsta understood fully and agreed to the terms of Chavez. "Say less, my friend. I'll send the text out." Gangsta pulled his phone out and sent the updated message to everyone.

"So, we will be en route to the meeting's place. I'll see you there, my friend," Loco said to Gangsta.

"Cool." Gangsta saw them to the door. He understood everything was protocol so it wasn't an issue with Chavez and his sudden demands. Gangsta also knew he was the head of the cartel's operation and he could not afford any fuck ups and disloyal shit, so he had a plan in place and he wanted to meet everyone so they too could be on the same page he was on.

He went back upstairs where Ne-Ne was still sitting on the bed in a daze. She tried to hide the fact by getting up from her bed and asking, "Everything good, baby?" She went to their closet.

Gangsta was still in love with the way she stood. Ne-Ne was still as bad as ever with age on her, and Gangsta knew he was blessed to have her as his wife. "Yeah, baby, everything so far is lovely," Gangsta said and took a seat on the bed himself.

She turned around and faced him. "So why is you having this meeting with everyone? Why are you dressed like this?" She pointed to him. "And why do I have this gut instinct telling me you are about to do something stupid?" Ne-Ne wanted him to answer those questions.

Gangsta didn't ever lie to his wife and she was the same. He looked at her for a moment before he finally said, "The meeting is just to update the made changes, baby. I'm not 'bout to do anything stupid. I'm dressed like this 'cause I was about to go do something stupid, but Kash did it for me so I came home."

Ne-Ne nodded to his statement then went back into the closet, doing whatever she was doing. Gangsta began taking his clothes off to get a shower real quick before the meeting. He wanted to be fresh and clean when he presented his next move. The game was still so unpredictable and vicious, so heartless and cold. Gangsta was far from soft and could run with the best killers around town. He was fearless and vicious himself, but today he was hurt by his true friend being killed and he vowed to never let another one of his friends lose their lives to the hands of greed.

Chapter 30
Veedoo

Him and his wife were out spending quality time with each other early morning. They were getting pedicures and foot rubs. The seats felt so good to his body. This particular shop did advance massages. It was a fairly big place with great staff.

Side by side, holding hands, Veedoo looked at his wife who was so beautiful and amazing to him. She still had that youthful look with natural hair. She had always been fine as wine and he was extra blessed to have a beautiful wife such as her.

Trish smiled at the look he held when looking at her. They always joked around with each other in public. People saw them and thought they were sister and brother until seeing them kiss or flirt. Veedoo blew her a kiss.

"Baby, let's make history this morning," Trish said to her husband.

Veedoo knew off top that this was one of her many jokes. He chuckled before asking, "Doing what?"

"Get your toenails colored red." She started laughing.

"Ha-Ha-Ha. Shut up, baby," Veedoo replied. He knew she always made lame jokes and he never got offended by it. He knew his wife had love and respect for him, so he didn't get bothered by her outbursts. Trish was as honest as they came. Everyone loved her personality and cherished her friendship. They all knew she liked to slide in jokes when off work. Now, when she's on the job she's very, very professional.

While sitting there, he received another text from Gangsta with a change of plans. Veedoo knew this wasn't going to be good. Now the meeting was taking place in the next hour. Veedoo shook his head in disbelief of the thought of telling Trish he had to leave their date when they hardly spent time with each other as it was. He knew she wasn't going to like this at all and he truly didn't want to say anything but he had to.

He took a deep breath and looked over to his wife once more. He knew it was better to tell her now and not later. Plus, it was no later. "Baby, I hate to stop our date but something very serious has overruled it. I'm sorry, baby," Veedoo said.

Instantly, Trish's face displayed sadness, hurt and disappointment; something he did not want to see. "No, bae!" Trish whined like a baby.

"I know, baby. It's business."

"So when do you have to leave, baby?" She was clearly upset by her pouting.

Veedoo didn't like this but he had to follow this text. He couldn't miss it. "Soon as we get done here, I got to take you home, but I'ma make it up. I promise. Soon, baby," Veedoo assured her.

Trish rolled her eyes. Disappointment was clearly on her face because their date had to be over so soon. She tried to seem convincing when saying, "I understand that but I'm working and I have a heavy case load right now, so this is like the only free time I will have, baby." Trish didn't want their day to end. It was just getting started and she was enjoying him too much.

Veedoo didn't want it to end either but he could not and would not miss this meeting. This was one call he couldn't miss and that was that. "Damn, baby, I hate it too but you know, with this business stuff—" He stopped talking and shook his head. This was the only statement he could make and eventually Trish understood the situation.

They had been married for seven years, and every year had been amazing. She couldn't ask for a better soulmate, and every day Trish thank God for him. Her family loved and respected him and that was extremely important to her. Veedoo felt the same way she felt and that's what made it amazing. He was a hood nigga that was blessed. Blessed to have the successful wife he had and the success he had gotten in the game. He was lucky and blessed.

After leaving the salon, they rode home together being that it was going to be a good while before they would have the free time again to spend with each other.

The music was low throughout the ride. Veedoo's mind was on what the meeting was about because when one such as this was called it's a serious matter. He also hated the fact that the time had been changed. Even though Trish knew all his friends, he still didn't want her to know he was ending their date for them or some of importance of one of them. It would make her think crazy and he didn't want that at all. Veedoo just hoped none of his friends decided to pull up to his home because that's how Gangsta had his operation going when it's a matter to meet about. Members of the cartel arrived together as one or in pairs. Veedoo just hoped he could make it home and leave before anyone made the move to come his way.

Jerry Jackson

Chapter 31
Montay

Montay and Pimp were standing inside a hidden room, looking at $9-million in cash when the text came through about the new meeting from Gangsta. He was surprised at how quickly the change was made. Montay would have to leave now if he was to make it. He was surprised by the time-frame to get there. It was within the next hour that he was supposed to be there. Montay knew the nearest meeting spot was Veedoo's crib which was a few blocks away. Anywhere else would be too far to travel. Pimp would have to take him there and drop him off if he was to make it in time. Montay pocketed his phone and started thinking of a plan to involve Pimp.

Pimp, on the other hand, was looking at all the money in his face. He had to move all of it from point A to point B, then he would have to put it up. His mind was still on the feds' harassment so he decided to ask Montay for a favor since they were into favors and shit.

"Say, bro, I need your contacts again, but not for murder this time," Pimp said out of nowhere, catching Montay off guard. He knew he would.

"Huh?" Montay's response was just that.

Pimp explained, "I need to see exactly what the feds got going on with a case on me. I figured if y'all can find out they watching me then you can get me the info of what they suspect I have done, 'cause the feds on me."

"Oh, I see, but I thought you already knew about the feds being on you." Montay was confused a little.

"Yeah, that was in Miami, though. This shit fresh here in Atlanta. My lawyer told me."

"Bro, the feds go state to state." Montay told him, just in case he didn't know, but Pimp knew and Pimp knew he was right.

"Yeah, but that investigation was tossed out is what I'm saying. I had put my lawyer on it, bro, and all he could tell me was that the government has a sealed case against me. I was asking if you could get me inside to see what it is or get it killed?"

Explaining it like that Montay then understand. "Now I see. Ah, yeah, bro. The man to holla at is Veedoo. His wife is a federal agent. Only thing about that though, you got to be cartel. See, being family gains you that protection, my nigga. I'm telling, ya. It's the best move for folks like us."

Pimp thought for a moment. He was right, and even though being in the game again was bad enough, now he would be under leadership. That was a big no-no for him. He was his own man and his own boss. He ran himself. At the moment, he had no other choice but to get with the program if he wanted help.

"I'm down," Pimp told him.

Montay smiled because Pimp was who they wanted with them anyway. "Good. We got this quick meeting right fast. I need you to drop me off, and while I'm there I'll holla at Gangsta. I know it's a go, I'm just saying we follow procedure, ya' feel me?"

"Drop you off now?"

"Yeah, just around the corner though. A few blocks."

Pimp agreed and got the keys to the safe house from Montay so he could come back to handle the millions. He already had a method of how he would do it. That was the simple part. Moving the money was the issue if any.

They left there and rode another 10 minutes, made some turns on side streets and ended up in a wooded neighborhood of large, expensive homes. Pimp made sure to note everywhere he traveled, no matter what. No matter where he went, he vividly remembered the location and direction. Montay directed him to a driveway of luxury cars and trucks. He pulled up behind a black SUV and instantly noticed the tag on the truck read government. Pimp didn't know if he was just paranoid or on point but that just didn't look right.

Before he could say anything about it, Montay spoke. "This Veedoo spot. His wife is a high official with the federal government. This how we stay safe." Montay got on the phone and made a call to Veedoo but got no answer. He then got out the car where Pimp stayed inside as he dialed into the phone again. When he turned, the gates came open behind them.

Another car pulled into the driveway beside them. Pimp instantly remembered Veedoo from the first meeting when he pulled up. He made sure to get a good look at the passenger who was a woman. When she got out of the car, the woman was beautiful. Pimp had to admit while looking at her after he acknowledged Veedoo with a head nod.

Veedoo was moving fast, clearly uncomfortable right now, and Montay peeped it. Trish got a quick glimpse of Pimp. They briefly locked eyes and she disappeared into the house.

Montay knew Veedoo was uncomfortable so he leaned back into the car with Pimp. "I'll catch you later, bro, and I got you on that, okay? Hit me if you got any type of concerns." Montay patted the roof of the car as Pimp backed up to leave.

Veedoo let his wife go into the house before looking over to Montay. "I wonder what this about 'cause I didn't like that encounter," he said then unlocked the doors to the bullet proof Benz they were to ride in.

"I don't know. Shit gotta be serious, though," Montay replied.

He and Veedoo hoped that Gangsta didn't call them to war with motherfuckers, or to even get into the grime of things because both men wanted out already. Neither man wanted to let Gangsta nor the family down, but the game was over with.

They got into the Benz and pulled out with little time remaining before the deadline to be there ran out. They would soon find out what was on Gangsta's mind, hoping to God it's just another update about the first meeting. Right now, neither wanted to be involved.

Pimp

He wondered if Veedoo's wife had anything to do with his case. Montay did say that she was high up, didn't he? And if she's not, then what? Does he get with the cartel for the protection of not being prosecuted? Could Veedoo's wife really save him?

One thing was for sure. If she couldn't save him and stop the investigation, then he would take them to war, both mentally and physically, and that was something he didn't want to do.

Pimp had one of his dad's contacts pull up all the names of the investigative agents on his sealed case. He had to pay a lot of money but it was well worth it, and he couldn't wait until the results came through. He had already made plans to execute every last agent's name listed. It would take grave effort and lots of energy. Pimp knew he could pull it off without a doubt.

While riding, Pimp never noticed the surveillance team that followed him through traffic. They had been on him since he left his house. The case against him was becoming stronger and stronger with passing time. They had so much solid evidence on Pimp and Honey already and he didn't even know it.

Pimp knew something though, and he was prepared at best. He would not let them stop him, slow him down or block him. If he had to murder every last agent responsible, he would do it. Their best bet was to leave him alone if they wanted to continue to live and enjoy life. That's all he wanted to do was live and enjoy his life, seeing his father free.

From the beginning of the grind in North Carolina, Pimp just wanted to get his father home. He had been in prison entirely too long for some bullshit. Pimp didn't care about the money, he didn't care about the fame, all he wanted was one man's freedom. Fuck everything else.

He was also in love with Icey and was about to be a father. All he wanted was to be happy. Pimp knew that if he handled his father's business, then became a husband and father, it would be an accomplishment. He was good with that picture.

Pimp's phone rung as he rode through the morning traffic. He looked and saw that it was Honey, so he picked up. "What's up, baby girl?"

"I don't know if I'm wrong or not, but I think I'm being followed," she said.

Pimp instantly knew what the feds were doing and why they were lurking, but how wondered how they knew. Somehow, some way, they found out he was involved, but how is the biggest question ever. He kept asking it rapidly to himself.

"Yeah, I figured that. Remember our lil' move back home in the North?" he asked. His mind was moving fast.

"Yes. Diamond's favorite," Honey replied.

Hearing Diamond's mans didn't faze him one bit. He showed no remorse at all. He said, "Okay, get with Yalonda and take that money with you. Go get your daughter."

Honey agreed without a second thought. She knew the heat was on and now Pimp was about to play his spread game. Her first rule was to lose all surveillance and get ghost because she would have to go into surveying mode. She would have to change her appearance and even her daughter's. That was the only thing Honey wouldn't like but she knew it was critical that she did exactly what Pimp so that his plan would work.

He hung up the phone with her and called his lawyer again to let him know what was going on. His lawyer was already in Atlanta, at the hotel. When he didn't answer, Pimp went there. He had no type of room to be slipping any more than he already had. He had to be on top of every little and big thing.

He was in traffic, looking around and keeping a keen eye out for anything out of pocket. Pimp was well-trained when dealing with methods of surveillance and security. He was well-trained in survival skills and knew how to physically fight in four different styles. It was unbelievable the amount of things Pimp had learned over the years of following his father.

After about ten minutes of driving, he finally peeped the surveillance team on him. They stuck out like sore thumbs. Pimp decided not to try and out run them. He would let them follow him to his lawyer's hotel room. He would then lose them because it was just that simple for him to do. As he drove, he switched his phone and took the chip out of his old one. He drove through downtown Atlanta in heavy traffic with his eyes on the feds who were following him. He cut the old chip.

He cut the new phone on, then texted his contact and his aunt, which would automatically give his father the new info. Within minutes his line rang a text message. It was the list he had been waiting on to see exactly how many agents he would have to murder.

The first name he read was a Latrisha Williams as the head in command. He kept strolling through names he didn't know. Then he saw Brad's name, which confused him. Pimp was baffled. *What was his name doing on the list? Is he the one who got this entire investigation going?* He had to tell his lawyer.

Pimp pocketed the phone after he counted 39, agents including those who worked in forensics on his case. A great idea came to his mind but he pushed it to the side. He continued to watch as the feds followed close behind him. He remained calm and wanted to make it to his lawyer.

Chapter 32
Trish

It was back to work for her this morning since her and Veedoo's date was interrupted by his sudden meeting and she was still upset by it coming to an end. Trish saw one of his friends and hated that she did. It just pissed her off more.

She was inside her office, putting all the correct paperwork together for the Savarous Jones case. Things were looking good and the team was getting somewhere with the case. Truthfully, she would rather be with her husband, enjoying his company, smelling his scent and seeing his handsome face. Yet, business was important, he said. Trish always understood his work and she respected his business, but when seeing his friends—the same people that nearly cost her, her job because she risked her job for love because of them—it made her mad all over again.

Even though she vowed to never do it again, she still had to accept the friendship Veedoo shared with them. She just disliked it and she told him this. Overall, she had met everyone and always keep it cool with his friends. She didn't ever go at them. She just hated to see any of them because it was like she knew they had dealings in the streets, and most likely they would have Veedoo in the streets. Drama came with them. She hated this fact, and so far, Veedoo had done good during the years they'd been married to keep his friends out of sight. Today, when she arrived at home, her mind was so caught up on the case that she even thought she saw Pimp at her house with one of Veedoo's friends. She could only get a glimpse of him, but nothing good enough. So, she let it go as Veedoo saw her into their home.

Her phone on the desk rang which startled her, making her jump from her daydreaming state of mind. She composed herself and answered as professionally as she could. "Mrs. Williams, commander speaking."

"Mrs. Williams, we have a positive match of bomb material with the van rented from the girl," one of the agents told her which brought light into her day.

Trish smiled. "Good, sir. Good work. So, you're saying that the van rented by the girl has residue of the material from bombs?"

"Correct, ma'am. Also, we have witnesses who put Pimp at the double homicide scene at the mall where the senator's daughter and boyfriend were gunned down. He actually has footage of the shooting on his phone. We have it being processed now."

She was elated that everyone was working. It was almost as if Pimp gave them the whole case.

"Great. I need to bring up an indictment. We have more than enough to get the ball rolling to arrest him and the girl. How is surveillance?" She asked excitedly.

"We have a team on Honey, Pimp and also his house. We were success at the bug we placed inside Icey's car, yet he hasn't got inside. At the moment, he's meeting with his attorney. He knows we're on to him."

"It doesn't matter if he knows or not. We have him in the web," Trish assured the agent. She was more than confident.

"Yes, ma'am."

She hung up the phone and went back to looking over other paperwork, smiling to herself. Just when she had thought the case was getting weak, it made a tremendous turn for the good. She couldn't believe how much evidence they had attained so quickly. It was all coming together just right for the team. Trish was proud of that.

As she sat there and read over paper's, she decided that after this case she would take her vacation. It would be right on time for her and Veedoo to take a much-needed break from everything around them. She missed him already and became jealous of the fact that he was with his friends instead of spending time with her.

She put the paper down on her desk then picked up the phone. She dialed her boss who picked up on the third ring.

"Yes, Mrs. Williams?"

"I'm ready to arrest both Lisa and Savarous," Trish said to her boss. She needed to get Veedoo off her mind.

"Draft me up a brief. If it's good, I'll take it to the judge and get it going," her boss said to her surprise.

"Okay, sir. Will do." She knew the protocol. She just wanted to see if her boss had any advice or demands of the case, but he didn't and Trish most definitely liked that.

She hung up the phone and stood up from her desk. She put her feet back inside the pumps she wore to walk out the office. She needed the results from the lab on the paperwork signed.

One thing about Trish, she always did things the correct way. that's why she was head over this case and many more. This case was open and shut like no other.

Pimp. She just hoped he didn't try to run or worse, which was to put up a fight that would turn deadly. All she wanted was justice served for the many people killed at that funeral. Pimp was dead wrong for what he did and Trish vowed to make him pay.

Jerry Jackson

Chapter 33
Brad

Brad was just getting up and out the hotel. The evening sun shined bright as traffic went by in a flash. He walked outside of his room and stretched his arms in the air, not knowing he was being watched by Pimp.

He had switched up on the feds. After leaving his lawyer, Pimp had left the five-star hotel on foot. He managed to sneak around surveillance and jump the bus. Now, he was watching Brad's every movement. The plan was to survey Brad the entire day. He would kill him later tonight or probably the next day. Right now, he had to see for himself the routes Brad took, who he met, and when he went to a place, Pimp needed to see what information he was getting and who he was getting it from.

Brad was ready to get his day started. First, he needed his coffee. He climbed into his car and found the nearest coffee shop. He had to have his wake up. Checking his phone, he saw messages from his mother, Icey and the office. He returned each text as he drove, not knowing he was being followed.

Today Brad had plans to comb the area where Pimp lived and he also wanted to see the first witness he ever met. He still needed her on the case.

Brad's phone rung. He saw that the caller ID read Icey's number so he picked up. "Hey, beautiful."

"How are you doing today?" she asked.

"I'm doing great, baby. About to start work. What's up with you?" It was killing Brad to be so fake with his best friend but this case against her boyfriend was very important, especially if Pimp was the person who bombed the church.

"I'm good. So when is the funeral for Jimmy?" Icey jumped straight to the questions. She badly wanted to show her support. She'd grown to know and love Jimmy which made it hard to not care and pay her respects.

"Oh, it's tomorrow. Sorry I didn't send over the director. You can ride with me unless you and your mother are coming," he told her because he knew that was what she was most likely talking about.

"Okay, that's what I was about to ask."

"Cool. And how is the baby?" He hated to ask that question. He was wishing like hell that Icey didn't have that baby, but she was so blind by love and now it was too late. It truly hurt Brad to know he was about to put her baby's daddy behind bars for a very long time. It crushed him every time he thought about it. He wanted his friend happy, true enough, but Pimp wasn't the right one for her. His life would eventually get her caught up or worse. Hurt or killed.

Brad could not imagine seeing this happen, that's why he proceeded to get Pimp and try his best to keep her in the blind. He was walking out the coffee shop with the phone to his ear.

"The baby is good. I'm due in four months, and guess what? Pimp is having me an entire school built."

He could hear her joy. It crushed Brad even more so much that he had to shut his eyes. He too knew that at the end of the day what he was doing was right. He was saving her life. She just couldn't see it that way.

Brad went to the headquarters to meet up with his new partner. When he rode into the parking dock, Pimp stopped following him and went past. Brad parked his car. He took a big sip of coffee from the cup. He had plans to get a lot of ground covered today because Jimmy's funeral was tomorrow and his entire family would be there. The last thing Brad would want was Jimmy's family thinking he didn't care.

He made it into the busy office, and the first person he saw was Trish, looking as good as ever. He couldn't help but stare at her standing over the fax machine. Brad knew she was a married woman and he wanted to respect that, but he just couldn't accept the fact. He wanted her himself, no matter how it sounded or seemed. Trish didn't pay him any attention as she did what she was doing. Brad, not wanting to be caught lusting after her, went about his business. He found his partner in their shared area. He was on the phone. The young agent held up a finger to tell Brad to wait as he continued to listen to the person on the other end. Brad sat his coffee and car keys down on his desk, then cut his computer on and pulled his chair out to sit down, never taking his eyes off his partner.

Moments later, the young agent hung up the phone. "We have surveillance of Pimp behind the funeral home. The guy's just now coming forward because he was afraid. I assured him that everything was okay, and that's when he agreed to meet."

This news alone made Brad's day begin even better. He was loving the moment. "So, when will we arrange that?" Brad wanted to know how the young agent handled himself.

"Now." The agent stood up as he grabbed his coat. "I have the address to where he is."

Brad smiled as he went to his computer for a quick note and to shut it back down.

Trish passed the guys on her way to the office. She gave that bright smile she had and spoke. "Gentlemen."

"Lieutenant. Ma'am, how is it going?" Brad spoke back.

"Everything is going well so far. The case is moving smoothly," she replied in walking.

Brad and his partner walked out the office. It was a good day, and as Trish stated the case against Pimp was moving smoothly. She was so happy to be close to the arrest of this monster. The agents had a glow on their faces. Neither knew Pimp was following them step for step.

Jerry Jackson

Chapter 34
Honey

The very next day, Honey was in North Carolina with Yalonda, doing as told. She had work to do and it had to be done fast. Yalonda picked her up from the bus station.

Honey got into the running SUV and closed the door. "Hey, girl," she spoke.

"Hey! Now, tell me what's going on with this boy." Yalonda wanted to know. Knowing wouldn't change anything though. She just wanted to know if her assumption was correct or not.

Being there for Pimp was a given. She would always have his back no matter what, when or where. Honey took the quick second to fill her in on the details of Atlanta. It didn't surprise Yalonda at all as she drove to her safe house Pimp had for them that she'd never been to. Today would be the first time she would be going.

Honey wasn't too worried about her and Pimp. She was more worried that Pimp would not succeed in getting his father out of prison. She knew this was his passion and was his everyday thought. If he couldn't make it happen, it would kill him. Everyone who knew Pimp knew this important part of him, and if you were anything close to him, you were his help.

All Honey wanted was to be there for Pimp at his time of need like she'd always been. She was his angel. She would forever protect him.

"His father's lawyer is talking good news, last I heard," Honey told Yalonda.

"It's about time. Honey, I swear I'm so ready to see him get out," Yalonda replied while sitting in traffic.

"Hell yeah. For all the money and effort he put into this shit?"

The girls rode the rest of the ride in silence with their minds on Pimp and his wellbeing. They had a certain type of love for him and it bothered them to witness him go through any type of hell. The ride was two hours outside of North Carolina, in a wooded area. The safe house looked like a cabin at first glance, but upon further inspection you could see that the wood-like home was actually bulletproof steal. Pimp had the place hooked up to the max.

Honey was in awe at the sight of the place. Yalonda entered the code and gained access to the ground. She rode up to the house slowly taking in all the view of the place.

The first thing Honey did was dye and cut her hair. She went from a brownish color to a full blonde, short style. She knew once her daughter came to Carolina she would to have to change her appearance. Yalonda had left her there to go handle shit and put things in place for Pimp. Honey was drying her hair while walking around the place, just looking taking in what she saw. She realized that Pimp had already planned this. The home was well equipped with all types of high-tech stuff. She was amazed to see all the shit Pimp had put together. He was actually ready for a mini war.

It took her a good hour to complete her hair and makeup. She also wore a booty pad that made her already fat booty look even better. She wanted to throw the feds off the next time she saw them because they were about to see a lot of her around town, whether they liked it or not.

Pimp had everything she would ever need. Honey turned on her new phone and reached out to her mother. She knew the feds would be on to her in a few so she chose to move faster than them. She just wanted to tell her mom what to expect when and if the feds pulled up so she wouldn't panic.

She chose one of the low-key fast cars with light tinted windows just in case. Pimp had her a fake ID and license that had a new name on it, which was practically a new life. She wasn't worried about it though. She was down with Pimp no matter what.

"Hey, ma." Honey spoke when hearing her mother pick up the phone. "Where is dad?"

"He sleep, baby, and how are you? I'm making it," her mother said. She was always happy to see or hear from her daughter.

"Good. Well, listen. Straight to the point, the FBI may come try to question you about me. Just don't help them, never. I'm not hurt nor in trouble. I'm just telling you what's up just in case, ma."

Honey had always had that relationship with her mother where she could be completely open.

"Lord have mercy, Honey. What's going on, baby? Please tell me, where is my grandbaby at?" her mother asked.

"I'm picking her up tomorrow, and ma, I told you I'm okay. I'm not in no trouble, okay?" Honey had to reassure her mother because she would worry herself to death.

"Okay, baby. I just hope you not telling me what you think I need to hear. And another thing, woman don't you ever question my love and loyalty with you. I'll never go against my child." Her mother checked her good.

It got a smile out of Honey as she drove and listened. She stayed on the phone with her mother another twenty minutes, then she ended the call when she got to the location where Pimp wanted her. She parked in front of a beauty salon while Nevea came out with a large bag over her shoulder. She had a phone glued to her ear when she got in the car with Honey.

Neither girl knew the other personally but both knew of each other, being that they were from North Carolina. They were connected with Pimp in some form. Nevea continued to talk on the phone but acknowledged Honey.

Honey lightly waved back. She had to help grab the big bag Nevea brought and put it into the backseat. Moments later, Nevea passed her the phone.

Honey pulled off and spoke. "Hello?"

"Baby girl, how are you?" It was Pimp.

She was happy to hear his voice. "I'm straight, baby. Wassup with you?"

"Lurking, baby. I have found out a lot of shit. We Slipped big time. I can fix it though, baby girl."

"Good, but I know that already, baby. I'm just surprised by us slipping, that's all," Honey said.

"So, take that money back to the spot. Go 'head. Pull up on the store so Nevea can handle business for Dontae."

She agreed by passing the phone back and continued to the next mission.

Jerry Jackson

Chapter 35
Pimp

He and Montay met again at the loft. He had an answer for Pimp about the business. Pimp got there and entered the place. It was a few GF niggas sitting around and Montay was coming in from the kitchen.

He had in his hand a glass of water. "What's up, brother man?" Montay said when he saw Pimp there.

"Shit, man, just making it. What's the move?" Pimp asked.

"Come walk with me." Montay knew not to discuss nothing in front of folks. He knew how Pimp was when it came to business. They walked into another room.

"What's up?"

"So, I spoke with Gangsta. Kash was there too and they understand. Only if you were a part of them could you gain the protection needed. No amount of money is worth it to them. It's not the money."

Pimp knew it would end up being something like that but he had another question. "What's Veedoo's wife's name?"

Montay didn't answer. He looked at Pimp a moment's, hesitant to speak. Simultaneously, him and Pimp were good friends, right?

Pimp was solid. "I got names of the investigations' officials on my tail."

Montay was stuck. "Her name is Williams, bro, but don't try nothing stupid like I know you will do. Let Gangsta handle it. Him and the entire family will meet tonight with you. You straight, bro, just fuck with the family."

Pimp's back was against the wall. He had to go ahead and agree to meet with the cartel, but if they couldn't pull it off, then he would be forced to take them out because it was no other choice left.

"Say no more. I'm there. Just drop me the details." Pimp agreed. He had no other choice but to comply. He knew how to be a team player and follow orders, he was just a leader.

"So, we good on that money?" Montay asked about the $9-million he gave Pimp.

"Yeah. We smooth," Pimp replied. His mind was on some bigger shit than money. His phone started ringing in his pocket. Pimp pulled it out, seeing his father's lawyer. With respect, he excused himself from Montay and picked up. "Yes, ma'am?"

"What I tell you about that? I have outstanding news."

"Yes. I need good news." Pimp pumped his fist and paced the floor as Montay watched.

"Your father has been approved for court," the lawyer said.

Her words sent chills down his spine. "When?" Pimp continued to pace the floor.

"The motions are in so I'm waiting on the response from the DA."

"When should that be?" Pimp wanted to know everything.

The lawyer laughed and said, "Come to my office I'll tell you." She never quit.

Pimp wasn't with the games right now and usually he would shyly flirt back. This just wasn't the time nor the day for flirting. "I'm serious."

The lawyer sensed his quick attitude and got professional with him. He paid her millions of dollars for this moment. It wasn't for her to celebrate, it was for his father and all the ground work he put in over the years on this mission.

"I should hear from the courts no later than two days, Savarous, sir," she said.

That was good enough for Pimp. He removed his attitude and got formal with her. "Okay. Thank you, ma'am." He hung up the phone, happy with the news. He pocketed the phone then looked at Montay. "I'll be there."

Montay agreed and walked him to the door after giving him the address to the meeting place.

Trish

She walked with a fast pace and her head held up high while she was in stride out of the office of her boss. Trish was clearly pissed. It was painted on her face like art that she was mad, but she tried to hide it.

Her boss just shut the indictment down, saying, "That's all circumstantial evidence. His lawyer will laugh at us. I need more."

Trish couldn't believe what she heard. She was literally about to go crazy in the office but she held her composure. She took the shut down and left. She just knew that she and the team would have to get more than just some he say, she say. They needed solid evidence before they could arrest Pimp. It shattered her hope but didn't stop anything. At the same token, she and the team had worked so hard, and to be shut down so easily was painful. She really didn't want to take the news to them that all the hard work was nearly in vain.

She made it out to her car and got in, then silently said a quick prayer for strength. Afterward, she calmed her nerves and crank up. Veedoo crossed her mind at that moment and all she wanted was her husband right now. She needed to be in his arms for comfort. She had the need to be treated like a baby and her husband was the only person capable of doing so.

Trish pulled off from the office. *A good cold soda is what I need*, she thought. The phone on her hip started to ring. She looked at its caller ID and saw it was one of the agents that were assigned to surveying Lisa, AKA Honey. Trish hoped like hell it was not bad news. She couldn't process more messed up news.

She answered. "Yes?"

"Hey, ma'am. I haven't seen any signs of life in this house since being here," the agent told Her.

Trish's worst nightmare was about to happen. She tried not to panic and thought logically first. She felt it was impossible for the Honey to just disappear. She didn't know she was a suspect. Or did she? "How long have you been on post?" Trish asked the agent.

"Nineteen hours, ma'am."

That didn't sound good at all. Panic started to set again. Her mind was racing against the possibility.

"Okay. Stage two. See if you can get a visual. If not, we will send someone over." It was the best step to go to.

"Okay, will do," the agent replied.

Trish didn't think Honey was gone. She decided to call the survey team on Pimp to check the progress with him. The agent she called at the office was a woman. "Commander Williams speaking. Surveillance on Jones. Give me updates," Trish told the agent.

"Okay. Savarous and his wife were followed throughout yesterday. They went home after being out for three hours. Savarous went back out and was tailed to his lawyer's hotel in downtown Atlanta, then he lost us. We reconnected visual at 11:30 that night. He left the house this morning at 8:56. We lost him at 9:01 and then connected again at 1:45. He's home now with his wife." The lady was very professional how she handled it.

Trish was baffled at the fact that Pimp lost the surveillance team. She wondered what he was doing. "Okay. Continue to work. Let me know when they leave. I'm sending a team inside his home to plant some bug."

"Okay, ma'am. I'll contact you as soon as it's clear."

Trish turned into a gas station so that she could get a soda. She pulled in and got out at the front of the door. The big question for her was where had Pimp been going. What was he up to? Yeah, she would need a serious vacation after this case. She needed her mind to breathe and rest. She needed her Veedoo. That's what she needed.

After she grabbed her drink and paid for it, she called home to see if he was there.

"Hello?" Veedoo used his deep, sexy voice when he picked up.

Trish smiled and she bit her bottom lip. "Can I come home and get fucked?" She surprised herself when it came out but that's exactly how she felt at the moment.

Veedoo didn't waste not a second giving her an answer. "As long as you let me taste that pussy first," he said.

That did it. "I'm on my way home. I'm officially still at work though, baby."

Her husband understood exactly what she was saying. "I'm waiting."

Chapter 36
Veedoo

Veedoo was at the house going over contracts and agreements on property and lands in other states when his wife called him on some spontaneous shit. One thing about it was that Veedoo loved the fact that his wife was a freak and they always pleased each other that way. Their sex life was amazing from the first time to the last.

Going through paperwork his mind reflected on the meeting they had with Gangsta. Gangsta had switched up the entire movement of the cartel. He put everyone in another place, and surprisingly he fired all Shooters and security. Veedoo couldn't figure why he did that but he said nothing.

He remembered Gangsta's words. "We don't need all that. We businessmen, and when the time permits then we will handle anything that comes our way. No parties. No gathering around. No ghetto, street shit. We are family men who has to raise their kids and lead their family, so we're gonna act accordingly."

He was more than happy that Gangsta left him in the position he was in because he truly wanted out of the drug business. His wife was with the FBI. He didn't need that anywhere around them.

Gangsta wanted everyone to report to him the smallest issues. He wanted all money to get processed through Montay and he gave Kash full control over the drugs. He gave Veedoo full control over all bank account details for every business they had. Veedoo was cool with that because it was easy, and his wife really had nothing to say about that type of business. It was bad enough he had millions of dollars that his wife didn't even know about that he would someday have to figure out how to get in their accounts.

While sitting there going through paperwork, he heard his wife's car pull up outside because his office sat right by the driveway. He shut the computer off to meet her at the front door.

Trish left her badge, gun and anything that had to do with her job inside the car. The only thing she had was her phone and a wet pussy as she approached her front door.

When she walked into the house, Veedoo was standing there. She blushed because he was looking so serious. Veedoo pulled her into his arms as she closed the door. He pinned her against the wall and kissed her lips roughly. Softly, he sucked her tongue and she did the same.

Veedoo lifted both her hands over her head, then ran one free hand down her neck and her chest. He continued to work his hand down to her slacks where he gripped them and her panties. He pulled them down while declining into a squat position.

Trish was already in heaven. She loved when he took control over her like he was doing. Veedoo kissed her pussy and rubbed her some. She was wet from the moment she walked in the house but now she was dripping. Veedoo slipped his fingers into her pussy to finger fuck her, and flicked his tongue over her clit. Trish wanted his fingers deeper. It was like he was teasing her. She kind of squatted so that his fingers could go deeper.

Veedoo pulled his whole hand away and stood up. He was face to face, nose to nose, lip to lip with her when he said, "That pussy taste so good."

He started patting her pussy. The sensation felt good. Trish's pants and panties were at her ankles. She kicked out of them and Veedoo led her to the sofa where he laid her back and got on his knees.

Trish had always had one of them very pretty pussies. It was a two-tone brown and pink but set just right. Her pussy lips were fat and her clit sat perfectly. She also kept it neatly trimmed and extra fresh. Veedoo opened her pussy with two fingers. She was pink and wet. He licked her juice just to taste her flavor again. Trish let out a moan as he then slowly, but with a great pleasure, started to suck her pussy lips, her pussy hole, and her clit finally. He moved his tongue in a slow circular motion with applied pressure. He then would suck hard at times on her clit and flick his tongue fast while eating her slow with passion.

Trish was in a trance of love and affection. She was so far gone in ecstasy. Veedoo was sucking her pussy real good. She couldn't help but reach down and encourage him to keep up the good work. Trish rolled her hips, rotating her pussy into his soft but firm mouth.

Veedoo slipped his fingers across her pussyhole and then down to her asshole. One finger went inside her as she felt his tongue enter her pussyhole.

"Yes, baby, yes," she moaned, still grinding but now on his finger and tongue.

He worked her like that then he completely stopped. Veedoo stood up. He was 6'4" and was as black as the night's sky with a ripped body that Trish was so in love with. He looked down at his wife with pure lust as he unbuckled his belt and unzipped his pants slowly. His lips were coated with her juices.

Trish stared and started playing with her pussy. She was opening it and seductively rubbing on it. Veedoo pulled his massive dick out first and bounce it at her. It was heavy meat she lusted after. He pulled his pants completely off and got back down on his knees back between her legs. He went back to sucking and licking her pussy.

"Lord, baby, yes. It feels so good. Baby, yes," Trish moaned, reaching out to grab his head again.

It wasn't long before she started to get into it and focused. She was on the verge of cuming. Veedoo was sucking her clit into his mouth and making his tongue rub across it forcibly.

"Babbbbby! Ohhh, baby, please! Oh weeeee! Baby! Oh my goodness! Oh, God! Baby, I. Baby, I am 'bout to. Ohhh!" Her body jerked and locked up as he fingered her pussy good.

After she had calmed down, Veedoo started kissing his way up her stomach, to her breast and sucked her nipple into his mouth. "I love you, girl," Veedoo said and kept kissing on her, moving up her body.

"I love you too, baby," Trish through a moan, then quickly let out a pleasure-filled moan when feeling his warm, hard dick. She felt every bit of him inside her walls. They had been married 7 years and still she couldn't take the dick.

Veedoo didn't ever try to hurt her either. He knew how to stroke the pussy just right with his size. "Damn, girl. You feel so good."

Veedoo started going in and out of her pussy slowly with just an up and down motion.

Trish put her hand on his hip and pushed to keep him from getting out of hand with her because she just couldn't take it. Veedoo put a hand out on either side of her. He turned her body to where her lower back hung off the sofa. Both his feet were planted on the floor. He held his wife by the hips.

She protested. "No, baby—"

"Yes. Yes, baby. I promise not to hurt you, woman; you hear me?" Veedoo asked her. He was looking directly in her eyes while he stroked her pussy with two or three inches.

It was so good that she felt herself about to cum again. She held on to his arm and his wrist as he was in and out her pussy, looking as sexy as ever. "Baby, I want you to cum," Trish said to him.

Veedoo instantly went just a bit deeper as he bit his bottom lip. "You want this nut?" He changed his strokes. Now he just let his dick sit up in her pussy as he rubbed her stomach. "Milk this dick, then, baby. Milk me."

Trish knew this was something that Veedoo liked when he wanted it. He didn't always demand this but when he asked for it, he wanted it with no objection. Trish put her feet on the floor and lifted her back off the sofa with his dick still inside her. She started rotating her hips. It was like her pussy was spinning on his dick and Veedoo loved when she did that.

"Um, yeah, bae. Good girl. Yeah, work that pussy. Make that dick feel good, girl. There youuuuuu. Yes, there you go," Veedoo encouraged his wife as she worked.

Trish slid up and down his long thick dick, twisting her hips and grinding. She felt him start to rock. She knew he was about to cum. "Oh you make me so wet, baby. Cum in this pussy, baby, while I cum on that dick," she said as she felt her own about to happen.

"Shit, bae, I'm 'bout to bust, girl." Veedoo grinded back as he felt the sensation of his nut pour out of him and into her.

Trish also was cuming hard as she continued to milk him. They were drained and sweaty. "Thank you, baby," Trish said.

"No. Thank you, baby," he replied.

They kissed deeply and got up. Trish had to go back to work and he too had work to complete.

"I'm 'bout to get a quick shower before going back out. I love you, baby," Trish said and headed upstairs.

"I'm 'bout to join you," Veedoo shot back as he followed. His phone rung. He pulled it out and saw that it was Gangsta. He continued to follow his wife and answered. "What's up, foo?"

"Say o'l hell going your way?" Gangsta asked as always.

"Just here with the wife. What's good?"

"Got another meeting tonight. I really need you to be there. It's very important."

Veedoo wondered what was it now. "Okay. Everything smooth though?"

They made it to their bedroom where Trish started getting undressed and he took a seat on the bed.

"Yeah, shit good. Just got to handle something with this new dude Pimp."

"Pimp?" Veedoo was confused. He hardly knew of this dude so why was he a part of a meeting?

"Yeah, I'll explain once you get here. It's at seven, brother."

Veedoo agreed. He hung up the phone and stood up to get undressed. He looked at his wife and her entire facial expression had changed. She was looking as if she had seen a ghost. "Baby, what's wrong with you?" Veedoo had to ask because she was looking crazy.

Trish made eye contact with her husband. "Oh, nothing. Just had a thought," she quickly replied and went into their bathroom.

Veedoo felt she wasn't being honest but he didn't say anything. He just stripped out of his clothes and followed her into the bathroom.

Jerry Jackson

Chapter 37
Pimp

He watched the federal agents lurk outside his home like they were being inconspicuous. It was serious but funny, Pimp thought. He was really just chilling until it was time to meet the cartel and he knew what the feds were doing. So, for right now, it was cool because their days are numbered.

Icey was gone with her punk ass best friend to the funeral for the fed that got killed. Nearly everyone would be there so Pimp would just chill for now. Lucky for everyone that Icey was there because Pimp would come out better blowing the entire building up with everyone in it.

He walked away from the window to take a seat on the bed where he pulled his phone out, making a call. He needed to put more actions into his plan.

Yalonda picked up the first ring. "Yes?"

"How we looking?" Pimp asked. He opened the laptop and turned it on.

"Two more days, it will be ready," she replied. That was good news to hear. "And she is a changed person," Yalonda added.

"Say less." Pimp was good with that info. He knew she was talking about Honey and her daughter.

"Anything else?"

"Yeah. I need you in Atlanta tonight. I'll text you details. Bring Nevea, too." Pimp started typing on the laptop.

"Okay. I'm waiting."

He hung up the phone, happy the plan was in motion and moving smoothly. He finished on the laptop and turned it off again. He was careful not to have things of such on around his house. Pimp knew the feds probably had already bugged his car; that's why he didn't talk in them when riding. He knew that nine times out of ten that his home was bugged as well. Even though he didn't talk like that, he was just still caution about certain things.

Pimp could only hope that Gangsta could get him saved by Veedoo's wife because, if not, things were really going to get ugly for the federal agents and their families. One by one he would brutality murder them in cold blood because they were asking for it, and Pimp had had enough.

Pimp had murder in his heart, in his mind, and in his soul. He was willing to kill everybody involved, no matter little or small. He didn't care if you were friends or not. At this moment, anybody could get it. Anyone except Icey. He had plans set in motion. He was waiting to push the button. He had everyone in place, ready to go on his command. Montay's best bet was to get this fed bitch to get off his case or else it was about to be a bloody Atlanta, Georgia real soon.

Trish

She was back at her desk, clearly still mad and bothered. The entire office building was empty due to the late evening funeral of one of their own, so it was extremely quiet there, leaving her to only her thoughts. She held a pen one hand and a motion to be signed in her other hand.

Trish had to stay and hold the fort down with piles of work in front of her face, but her mind was still stuck on the fact that she heard her husband talking to Gangsta and caught the mentioned of Pimp's name. Now, she knew without a shadow of a doubt that the man she saw in her driveway was Pimp.

This fact scared her because how could her husband have any dealings with this man if her husband wasn't in the game? Pimp, of all people, was at her home in some way, in some form connected with her husband. Was Veedoo hiding something from her? Was he in the streets again, running with his crew? She could only pray the answer to be no because if yes, she would be crushed.

Trish sat there in a daze. She could vividly remember how she jeopardized her job years ago to help Veedoo and his friends out of a serious federal case. She had gotten caught up like that one time and made a grave promise to herself that she would never do that anymore. No one could make her that weak again. She wasn't mad about the choice she made because in the end she got a wonderful husband.

Veedoo had also made promises to her, and one promise was to never put her in that predicament again because she did it through love and he knew this. He had promised to always protect her and step carefully in her best interest. He promised to keep the streets from around her and that he wouldn't bring anything illegal around her or their home.

She just prayed that he had the perfect excuse for this man Pimp being in her driveway, because for the soul of her she had thought of a million reasons why, but none seemed logic. She was for certain that was Pimp in the car driving and couldn't nothing convince her otherwise.

She also received intel that the girl Lisa, AKA Honey, was missing. A team of agents went inside her place and found it completely empty. Trish was forced to put out an APB on her. She needed her. Pimp was recorded being home so that was a good thing that the surveillance on him was holding up. She couldn't help but wonder what would be Veedoo's answer when she asked him about Pimp because she most definitely had to ask him. She needed to know. They had a good relationship and she just didn't think he would crush it for someone he just met. It was impossible. She knew her husband would not lie to her.

Jerry Jackson

Chapter 38
Pimp

Icey had yet to make it home and it was time for him to hit the streets. He had a meeting in the next three hours. Pimp decided to leave early because he knew he would have to lose the feds before he could get there. He walked outside to his G-wagon and got in to crank up, then pulled off.

He knew the tail was sitting two houses down. Pimp went their way on the opposite side, making them have to turn around. This is when Pimp put the pedal to the metal. The wagon went from 20 to 100 miles per hour in under 60 seconds down a calm residential area. He made a quick left turn and made the truck speed down another street.

He pulled out a remote as he made a right turn and raced up a hill. Looking in his rearview he could see the tail finally turn the street. Pimp was at the top of the hill. He pressed a button on the remote and kept speeding out of sight of the tail. He made a sharp turn into a driveway. The garage door was closing as the car slid into the open space.

Pimp jumped out and got into a black Ford Mustang with mirror tinted windows. He crank up and used the same remote but different button this time, and the garage door opened. Pimp pulled out the driveway and continued on with his mission. He cut the GPS on and typed in the location where he was to meet the cartel. His phone rung. He saw that it was Icey.

"Wassup, baby?" he answered.

"Hey, baby. What you doing?"

Pimp could tell she was out. He could hear people in the background talking. "Nothing much, baby. 'Bout to go meet this lawyer for my father. How are you holding up? How is my Junior?"

"I'm good and the baby is just perfect. We just ate a meal. I was calling to tell you that I would be out a few more hours, okay?" She sounded happy and he didn't want to mess that up.

"Okay, baby. Cool. We should walk in at around the same time. I love you," Pimp said as he drove and made sure to look for feds lurking in the traffic.

"Okay, baby. I love you too," Icey replied.

They got off the phone and Pimp locked in on his mission but he couldn't help but wonder about the conversation Icey was having with Brad. What were they talking about? Was it him? Was Icey going against him? Really, it didn't matter because Brad's days were numbered. Pimp had to have him because he was in on every play. He was doing entirely too much. Pimp following Brad had produced his witness, his leads and his resting place known as a safe house. He was good as dead and his witness too.

Pimp had him figured out from A to Z. He also had 60% of the other agents figured out too. He was just waiting on the outcome of this meeting before he pushed that button. Pimp was ready to get this whole situation out of the way. It was becoming a pain in the ass.

Would Icey cross me, he thought while driving. At times, he had to ask himself but then he realized that he would not give her that choice to cross him. He trusted her though he had to because love told him that he could, and he truly had love for Icey. Pimp just wanted his life to be smooth. Why do the federal government want to mess that up? His baby was on the way into the world. He didn't need this drama right now. He had a mind full of so many different things. He had questions and no answers but would soon find out. Whether he liked the answers or not, he had to know what was what. Pimp kept watching traffic as he drove. He would not slip anymore. From now on, he was on everything moving.

It took him 45 minutes to finally make it to the place where the meeting would take place. It was in Gwinnett county at a mansion that was surrounded by luxury cars of all kind. He pulled the Mustang GT up beside a Bentley. Pimp knew that security was out and would take his weapon, so he left his gun in place and got out the car to be surprised to see no Mexican guard or any type of security.

Pimp wondered if he was even at the right place. He looked around and wanted to go get his gun, but he kept walking up to the large doors atop the steps. Once he was on the porch, he knocked on the door three good times, hearing it echoing through the house even from outside. Within minutes the door began to open. It was a Mexican lady that was super bad.

At first, Pimp was stuck looking at how sexy she was, but he caught himself. "I'm looking for—"

"Gangsta. I know. Come in." She spoke perfect English to his surprise.

Pimp followed the fine Mexican girl through the well laid, expensive house until they reached a den area where everyone was waiting on him.

"There go the man of the hour right there." Kash was the first person to speak up. The entire room looked up to Pimp when he entered the room.

"My friend." Loco was making his way from across the room. He held his hand out for a handshake. Pimp shook his hand. "My friend, how are you?" Loco asked.

"I'm good, sir. You?"

"Blessed. Have a seat."

They took seats on the empty sofa. The room was full of mostly the same people he met the first time.

Gangsta nodded toward Pimp as he sat down. "Straight to the business. Didn't I tell you the feds was at yo' door step?" Gangsta began to speak he stood up. "But that's nothing we can't fix."

It sounded good. Pimp had to question what Gangsta was saying. "Yeah. I thought my lawyer had dealt with that shit in Miami and he did. That case is tossed out. It's not the Miami shit though, feel me? It's much bigger." Pimp had to be upfront and direct because he didn't need any misunderstanding of anything. He knew one thing about the cartel was that they handled good business. They had folks in high places working for them, and Pimp needed their resources.

"Help me understand what are you saying. The feds on you for some fresh shit that's deeper than the shit in Miami?" Gangsta wanted to know. Everyone wanted to know.

"Listen, I don't know where the shit coming from, but it's here in the city. Feds investigating me and my girl and everyone involved. They are assuming I'm the one who caused the bombing of the funeral. That's crazy," Pimp lied.

"Sho' is crazy. So you bombing shit, too?" Gangsta had to ask. Everyone was surprised at the situation.

"Hell nooooo, bro, that's not my thang. I'm just a nigga the feds want for any lil' or big reason. My baby mama best friend works for the feds and he hates my guts," Pimp told them.

Gangsta didn't expect this. Pimp had entirely too much going on. He looked at Veedoo who had a look of hate on his face. Gangsta hated the fact that he would even consider asking him to pull any string possible. He knew how Veedoo's wife put her job on the line to kill the case against them so it would be extremely hard to get her to side with them again.

"I hope not. Damn, bro. You in deep," Gangsta said after thinking a moment.

"I'm just trying to chill," Pimp said more to himself than anyone.

"That's why we told you to get with this shit from the start, nigga. We could've been had you stamped but you wanted to think this cartel shit ain't what's popping." Kash had jumped into the conversation.

"Nawl, it wasn't like that, my nigga. Told y'all niggas I just got out some issues. Montay could've told y'all niggas that," Pimp replied.

"I did," Montay spoke up for himself.

"Okay. See, I'm just telling y'all I have been through states of beef with niggas, murder charges and even some federal kingpin shit in Miami, and now this bomber shit. I just want a break." It was true that he was tired, but it was more like fed up than anything, especially with Brad's bitch ass.

Kash shook his head, looking at Pimp before he said, "So, I hear you can throw ya' hands good. You a lil' nigga you know they say hit hard. Is that true or false?"

"Could be true. I'm confident in my process," Pimp replied.

"You are well-trained in combat and survival skills. Any time in the field?" Loco asked him.

"Never." Pimp shot back quickly. "The temple." He looked at Loco who understood what he was speaking of.

"Where you from originally?" Veedoo finally spoke.

Even Pimp had to give him a strange look to hear him step up to the plate. He valued Veedoo's input on a lot of business issues. Pimp could tell Veedoo was feeling some type of way like he didn't want no part in this meeting. Pimp was good in reading people. "I'm from North Carolina," Pimp was proud to say. He too wanted to tell them to stop firing questions at him like he was some kid about to get into trouble. He just wanted their help, or at least for them to say that it's nothing that can be done so he could handle it his way.

"I mean, you know ya' boy be boasting and shit on ya' game. He say you took over the entire South Beach and Dade county. That's some nearly impossible shit, my nigga, but I'm saying can you pump one of my states like this?" Kash asked him.

Loco nodded. He liked the question.

"Bro, I can do all kind of amazing shit, but I'm not even trying to see that dope shit. I can wash some money, run some companies, but that—"

"Hold up, hold up. Ain't no demanding spots, playboy. It's the grind way, my boy. It's the best route. Don't be scared," Kash told him. If Pimp needed the help from them, then he would have to comply with what they had to offer.

"Just chill." Gangsta stepped in between Kash and Pimp. He had his hand on Kash's chest. "Let me handle the business." He looked his true friend directly in the eye, and best believe Kash knew what it meant.

"Say less." Kash put both hands up and backed up.

Gangsta turned to face Pimp. He walked a little closer and began to speak. He was different from Kash. Gangsta was humble when Kash was fierce and bold. "I'd love to help you out, brother, especially on the cost of Montay always speaking something good about you. But at the same time, not only am I a family man, I am also a multi-business owner, stamping myself as an extreme businessman. So, with that being said, my only payment is loyalty out of this situation. So, tell me. Can I gain that in full?"

Pimp looked at Gangsta, then to Kash and finally to Montay before he said, "I operate through loyalty. It's all I know and all I ever stand on. Like I said, I'll fuck with the team, but if you know like I know, then I need to lay low." Pimp needed the protection the cartel claimed to have, but he wasn't trying to sell his soul for it. They'd better know that much if they didn't know anything else.

"Understood," Gangsta said. He then looked to Veedoo, knowing what was on his mind. Gangsta made the necessary call right there. The phone rang a few times before a female answered.

"Hello?" Asia answered. She was one of his most loyal team players. She was the most solid he'd seen in any female.

"What's up, love? Question." Gangsta covered the phone with his hand and asked Pimp, "What's your name?"

"Savarous Jones," Pimp replied.

Gangsta went back to the phone call. "Savarous Jones. Check the files. See what's up."

"I'm on it, baby," Asia shot back and hung up the phone. Gangsta had put her in a position with the government. She handled all organized paperwork, meaning she saw everything. He turned his attention to Pimp again. "We will know exactly what's up in a minute or two. But, yeah, you will be cool, brother. Shit gonna get handled."

Pimp understood and nodded. He wanted badly to say something about Veedoo's wife being the case leader on his FBI file. He just didn't want to say anything first. He wondered how the cartel was coming. He didn't want to just show his whole hand like that.

Another five minutes had gone by and Gangsta's phone rang again. Everyone got quiet so that they could take in what Asia was about to say.

"Yes, love? I'm here." Gangsta put the phone on speaker.

Pimp heard this sexy voice say, "They have a sealed case on him. it's about that bombing at the church. Not only him but a Lisa too. They know about the van, they have video of Savarous around the funeral home, they have the girl renting the van. No prints or hard physical evidence though. This is why the first motion to indict and arrest him was not approved. Everything right now is circumstantial."

"Thank you, love."

"You're welcome," Asia replied and disconnect the call.

Gangsta put the phone in his pocket. "So, there you have it. They got you cornered but they don't really have shit on you, though. Good lawyer will eat that alive, and plus this saves us from having to go Veedoo's route."

"I want them to just. I thought you could put an end to this shit, bro. I mean, 'cause I can handle my business myself—"

"Listen, what we are saying is that if we don't got to pull our strings then why do it? Let's just let our law team tackle the case and see what's what?" Veedoo was the one that spoke.

"My friend, we will find a way out of no way," Loco added.

Pimp's mind was made up. He gave it his best shot. Nobody would stop him. Nobody would stop his mission and he meant that. As bad as he wanted to be cool and stay calm, it's always something pulling him back into this murderous game.

"Say less. So, what do I do; just hide?" Pimp wanted to know as he stood up to leave. He had only one thing on his mind.

"No. Just remain normal. We will handle it, my friend," Loco told him.

Pimp hung around another minute or two, then he left the meeting. Nightfall had just embraced the skies. It was perfect timing for Pimp and the vicious shit he was about to do.

Jerry Jackson

Chapter 39
Brad

He was returning from dropping Icey off at home after Jimmy's funeral. He was drained from standing up all day and talking with all the family and friends that showed up in support of Jimmy. Today was a sad day for Brad when seeing his partner being put to rest from being killed on duty. It crushed him but also motivated him to find the person behind this act. This crime wouldn't go unpunished.

Brad had to get it together. He was stronger than he thought, but right now it just didn't feel like it because he was still emotional from the funeral. He had to gather himself because he had work to do.

Jimmy would not die in vain. He won't let that happen. Pimp would surely pay for this one. If convicted, Icey would see the true him because, right now, she was still blinded by his love. Something Brad would never understand.

He pulled the car up to the townhouse he shared with his new partner. His car was there. Brad was glad to be home as he pulled alongside the car. Cutting the car off, he sat there a moment's time just thinking that he would be happy when all this was over so he could rest and sit back.

Icey wouldn't be so mad at him once she found out the truth of who Savarous Jones really was. Right now she couldn't be convinced that Pimp was the bad guy. She would not believe it if God said it himself that the man she loved was a ruthless killer.

He finally got out the car, leaving his gun and ID inside because he would be in and out. Brad closed the car door and proceeded to his shared apartment. He used his card key to enter the code first, then turned the lock. The door cracked opened. He entered and got the shock of his life.

The entire front room looked like someone had ransacked the place. The first thing Brad did was start to pull his weapon. A weapon he didn't have. He was about to run to the end-chair by the sofa to retrieve a hidden gun, but hearing Pimp's voice stopped him in his tracks.

"Bring yo' ass in and join the party." Pimp had emerged from the shadows. He and Brad made eye contact. He was looking like the monster he was with bloodshot eyes and his aim steady, not a glitch in his wrist.

Brad knew not to try anything stupid. He was stuck. He had no other choice but to comply because he didn't know the situation with his new partner. All Brad saw was that the front area was destroyed but there was no blood. "Where is my partner?"

"Oh, he in here. Come on." Pimp had the gun trained directly at his head.

Brad knew he couldn't make not one move. He started walking toward Pimp with his hands in the air. Pimp moved to the side to let him by. Brad walked to the bedroom cautiously, not knowing what to expect. He could only pray.

Brad's heart dropped to the pit of his stomach when he looked inside the room his partner slept in and saw him nearly ripped to pieces. Brad couldn't even turn around to face Pimp to question him or anything. He didn't feel or hear anything. All Brad saw was blackness. The bullet tore through his head and out the front before he could even react.

Pimp shot him three more times in the head and neck area. He stood there, looking down at the slain FBI agent. Pimp took the silencer off the gun, tucked it and made his exit. Two down with thirty-nine more to go, and Trish Williams was at the top of his list.

Pimp

It was around 10PM when he got the call from Yalonda and Nevea. They were in Atlanta as he requested. Pimp met them at the airport, picking them up in the front while driving a low-key car. Yalonda got in the front and Nevea got in back. Neither had luggage with them; just cellphones.

Pimp pulled off. "What's up, y'all?" he spoke while slipping into traffic.

"What's up, boo?" Yalonda spoke.

Nevea just waved her hand. They already knew exactly what they had to do once they got to Atlanta. Pimp had everything laid out. All they had to do was follow his plan to the T without messing up or be late to any point made. Pimp too had to make it home in time enough so that Icey wouldn't think nothing of him being out of her sight when Brad was murdered. So, he sped through traffic to get the girls to their place.

Without another word spoken, he drove both girls to the place where everything was set up for them. Tomorrow was going be a bloody morning. He was literally about to bring disbelief to the city of Atlanta. His plan was in full motion and it was no turning back now. He had already murdered seven more gents after Brad and his partner, and at least ten more would get the business tomorrow. He was all in. Pimp had tried to ease through but they woke up a monster they really didn't want to see.

When he got a few blocks away from his house, Pimp parked the car. He knew it was a surveillance team outside his home, so he would creep up on feet through the woods and sneak into the house. He knew that Icey was going to be crushed by her best friend being killed, and he knew he would have to console her through it. He was ready, too. *Fuck Brad. He got exactly what he deserved*, Pimp thought.

Icey was in the bedroom, wrapping her head for the night when Pimp entered the room. She saw him through the mirror and smiled, happy to see him. She hadn't seen him since this morning. Icey turned around on her stool. "Hey, baby," she said as she stood.

"What's up, baby?" Pimp pulled her into his arms for a kiss.

"About to get in bed."

Pimp began to take his shirt and pants off. He looked at his phone and saw that Montay had called three times. He tossed the phone onto the nightstand. "I'm tired too," Pimp replied. He was glad she was calm and cool. He went to the bathroom to shower before he would join her in bed.

Jerry Jackson

Chapter 40
Trish

She had to be dreaming. Wasn't she federal government? The real police? She was FBI, right? This couldn't be true. This had to be fake. It had to be a big joke out of nowhere. She couldn't believe this. It couldn't be true.

Trish stood in the threshold of one of her slain FBI agents' doorway. The crime scene was unbelievable. Whoever committed this crime had a personal grudge against the agent. The crime was too up-close and personal. Trish was crushed by these events and even more crushed as news continued to pour in of other agents who were also was murdered in their safe houses.

"Mrs. Williams? Williams! Hey! Ma'am, you okay?" Somebody said, which brought her out of the trance she was faced with.

Trish moved to the side as the crime scene was being taped off and processed. She looked at the person who was talking to her. It was her boss. "Yes. I'm okay. I'm fine." She had to get her mind together. She had to quickly figure out happened. What was this about?

"Okay. Well, it's no time for standing around. We got work to do so let's do it. Oh, and that Savarous Jones case is no longer a priority. This is," her boss said and stormed off with another elite team of agents.

Trish couldn't believe that someone actually killed ten FBI agents in one night. Without any more thought she entered the apartment of Brad and his partner. The place was a total wreck, she noticed, like it was a big struggle, a fight or something which could pan out to be good for evidence findings. Trish walked over to one of the agents she knew from the office. "Excuse me. I need updates ASAP. Any prints? Blood? Any physical evidence? Anything to go on yet?" Trish asked him.

"Nothing yet. All we can say is that they've been dead between six to seven hours," the agent told her which was no help.

She also knew that everyone had just arrived and was just now working. She could only nod and walk around the apartment. Trish had this thought of what her boss said before he left the apartment. He told her that the Jones case was over and that she had to shut it down. That bothered her badly because she had put too much work in for the case to be shut down. She understood though, being that so many agents had died. This entire event had everyone baffled. This was something that had never happened. It was history in the making.

The sun was just now coming up. The morning dew still coated front yards and sidewalks. She was leaving the crime scene because there wasn't much of anything to go off of, so she decided to go to another scene to see if the crimes had similarities in hopes that it did so they would know what they were dealing with.

The morning was a busy one. Nearly every street in Atlanta, Georgia was busy with the media, federal government officials and local cops. It was ten federal agents murdered within six hours on three sides of town. Trish knew not just one man was capable of doing this job. What she didn't know was how many people and the reason behind it. What caused this? She pulled her phone out and called one of the surveillance agents.

The phone rang a few times and the woman picked up. "Special agent Smith."

"Commander Williams speaking. Surveillance on Jones. Give me details."

"Surveillance on Jones and his girlfriend positively identifies Icey and Savarous' home. Still no sign of Lisa."

"How long have you been on post?"

"Only two hours, ma'am," the agent replied.

"So, who was the agent that released you? What's the call code?"

"Sorry to say, ma'am, he's one of the slain," the agent sadly said which surprised Trish, and she again wondered.

"Where did it happen?" She wanted to know, and was hoping like hell it wasn't at Savarous' home.

"Safe house, ma'am," the agent confirmed.

Trish was good with the news. Whether it being Pimp being a suspect, she was glad he was home and out the way. She continued to drive to the other crime scene and putting different scenarios together in her mind. She badly wanted to find out what was the reason behind this act of violence.

Pimp

Sleep wasn't anywhere near him as he continued to lay there in bed, looking at the ceiling fan and dim lights. Pimp looked and wondered how shocked Atlanta really was. How sad were ten different families? Pimp briefly looked over to Icey. She was still sleep in her own little world.

He reached over to grab the phone from the nightstand and saw that it was just 8:28. He had two miss calls, both from Yalonda and a text message. He opened the message and read it. She was telling him that she and Nevea were ready.

Pimp quickly jumped out of the bed and got dressed. He had no time to waste right now, being that Yalonda had already made her move. He didn't bother to wake Icey as he lightly kissed the side of her face. "I love you." He spoke lowly while looking down at the one he truly loved. He knew today that he would be taking the chance that could cost him his life, and this just might be the last time he'd ever see her again.

He made it outside to his driveway. Today, he decided to drive Icey's car. He knew surveillance was out and he wouldn't be trying to get around them. Today, he wanted them to follow, look and learn. When he pulled out the driveway and drove down the street, he was surprised to see that it was no agents sitting to the side, waiting to follow him. Pimp also knew that the feds were slick, so he kept a keen eye out for anything else as he drove out of Buckhead and into the inner city of Atlanta, into Fulton county. It took him 30 minutes to reach a laundry facility on Westlake Avenue. Pimp pulled the car around back and into a shop's garage.

When he got out the car he was greeted by an older dude.

"Follow me," the man spoke and led the way to a back room.

When Pimp entered the room, it was filled with all kind of weapons and armor. They kept walking into another room that was more clean and spaced out, Pimp noticed. Then, he saw Yalonda and Nevea sitting there as expected.

"Let's do it," was all Pimp said as both girls stood up to leave.

They all got into a black on black Benz two-door coupe. Pimp was the driver as he came out the front of the shop. Hidden behind dark tint, he hit the streets with the girls ready to complete the mission at hand. He picked up the phone and called Honey to see what was up with her.

She picked up the phone on the second ring. "Yes, I'm here in place," she said before anything else.

"Cool. I'm en route," Pimp told her which was another code to make another move.

Honey

She hung up the phone with Pimp and crank up the car she drove. Only around the corner from Pimp's house, she headed in that direction with only one thing in mind and that was murder.

Looking in the backseat she saw her daughter asleep, oblivious to the world and all its sinful acts. How could she put her daughter in this situation? Why was Pimp so important in her life? Was her own life even worth anything at all? These were unanswered questions she had.

Honey loved Pimp and she would risk it all for him. From the beginning of them to the end of them she was willing to go to hell and back for and with Pimp. She was pulling the car into his driveway after she passed the surveillance agent three homes down. The agents saw her but paid her no attention until she pulled into the driveway.

Honey looked different. She had black hair now instead of blond, and it was dreadlocks now instead of a sew-in. She did as planned and got out of the car. She walked to the backdoor to get her daughter out but then she stopped.

All at this time, Honey knew she was being watched carefully by the feds. She knew this was a part of the plan so she went back to doing what she was doing. She got her daughter out the car and stood her to her tiny feet.

"Come on, baby." Honey grabbed her daughter's tiny hand, walked out of the driveway and toward the federal agents parked on the side street. All for love she was out there with her daughter. All for love she was about to pull the unthinkable and risk it all. When she reached the car the two agents sat in, Honey stopped. She was more nervous than ever, especially the way the agents looked at her. "Excuse me this morning," Honey said as she peered inside the vehicle. It was a Male and female inside. The woman was the driver. Honey wondered if the agents were thinking like her. Did they notice how nervous she was?

One of the agents rolled the window down. "May I help you?" The man spoke.

Honey took the opportunity to let her daughter's hand go and reach into her bag. She pulled out a photo of Brad. She passed it to the agent. The man grabbed the photo. *It was now or never*, she thought as the woman and man looked down at the photo. Honey reached in her bag again but this time she was pulling out a gun.

Before the agents had a chance to react, Honey was shooting into the federal agents' car. All she could remember was seeing the bullets rip through each agent. The first bullet striking the woman in the face, the next six shots were into the chest and neck area of the guy. She reached inside the car and took both IDs.

Honey was more nervous than she'd ever been. She didn't realize the clip went empty until hearing her daughter brought her back to reality.

"Mommy!" The baby screamed as Honey tucked the gun, quickly snatched her child up in her arms and headed off in the direction of the car.

She just committed an unthinkable crime, leaving two federal agents dead in the car from multiple gunshot wounds.

She put her daughter in the car, got in, and just as fast she pulled off. She never saw Icey standing in her living room window, looking at her every move. Honey pulled off and called Pimp to let him know she was headed to the next place.

"Say less," was all she heard him say, and the phone went dead.

Chapter 41
Pimp

It wasn't impossible to get inside this FBI crime lab but it was very hard to get past a certain security which was the ID badge of each agent. Both Yalonda and Nevea had those ID cards from Honey, leaving them at a location. Pimp dropped the girls off at the building downtown where they were to go in as agents and slip into the utility room, then hide in the ceiling until the place closed.

Pimp had other things to do while the girls got into place. His phone started ringing. He looked and saw that it was Icey. "Hey baby, what's up?" Pimp picked up. He was hoping that she didn't get the news yet of Brad, but hearing her crying on the other end made his hopes wash away like water and soap.

"My friend is dead, baby! Someone killed Brad, baby! Something is going on, Savarous. Two more FBI agents were just murdered on our street. The killer parked in our yard!" Icey cried.

Pimp hated that. She was his pride and joy and he hated the fact that he was the reason behind her hurt and her pain. He hated it bad but he had to do it just like he had to console her. "Damn, baby. I'm sorry to hear that. I'm just at my father's lawyer's office doing paperwork. I can be there within the next hour, or do you want to meet me here?" Pimp tried to sound concerned.

"I'll meet you there, baby. I do not want to be around all this killing," Icey cried

"I got cha, baby, I'll be here."

Pimp knew he had to get to the lawyer's office fast because he still had to handle business in the streets, but that's where she expected him to be. He had to make things quick because he had more agents to murder and Trish was top of the list.

He was in traffic when he and Icey hung up the phone. Yalonda and Nevea should by now at least be past security. He was pretty sure they were because he told them to call if they couldn't get past. They hadn't called so they had to be on the inside already, he estimated. Pimp drove fast through traffic so that he could beat Icey to the lawyer's office and grab some papers. He knew everything had to be looking right because Icey wasn't easily fooled and this was one crime he could never admit to.

Brad should have stayed in his place and he would still have his life. Trish should have stayed to herself because she too would have her life. But no. she wanted to be the head commander that brought him down. Veedoo should have put a leash on his bitch because now she was about to pay with her life. A debt owed to him. He hated that things had to be like this but it wasn't nothing in the world that could stop him and keep him from doing whatever it took to succeed in his mission.

Pimp was willing to die to make good on his promise to see his father free from prison. He'd spent his entire life growing up being programmed to this mission. By the age ten, Pimp had been to places and learned valuable lessons from each. Pimp had done things at that age a man hadn't done his lifetime. This mission he lived and breathed its success, and was willing to die to get it.

After calling his father's lawyer, Pimp made it to the office in the next twenty minutes. When he entered the nicely furnished office, he was met with her secretary. "Mrs. Gwen will now see you," the woman said and waved toward a double door.

Pimp already knew exactly where her office was so he walked into the room to find the lawyer laying on the ground, doing sit ups in workout attire.

The lawyer stood to her feet, looking Pimp directly in the eye and spoke. "What can I do for you, Mr. Jones?" She was being professional.

Pimp saw that she was being personal, though he saw her every emotion. She still felt some type of way about his statement. She couldn't hide this fact. Pimp closed the door behind him and pulled out a bankroll of money. "My girl is on her way up here. I need you to front with me. I told her I was up here doing paperwork. She just had a death in the family so she's in an emotional state. I need you to give me some paperwork to fill out, so that's what it looks like I'm doing when she gets here," Pimp said and counted out three grand. He tossed it onto her desk.

The lawyer just looked at the money, then up to his face. She finally had him where she wanted him and the funny thing is that she did not want him or it anymore. She did have to remain humble and professional at all times though because Pimp had invested well over $3-million cash into her and she loved his money. Loved it so much that she pocketed the three grand.

"Take a seat. What time are we looking at before she should arrive?" the lawyer asked.

"She should be here any moment now," Pimp replied.

The lawyer nodded and went find the proper paperwork for him to begin filling out.

Icey

Hurt wasn't the word. Crushed wasn't the fact. She was beyond all of that right now. She was broken and let down. Her dreams and hopes shattered like glass as blood drained from her body.

Icey had always been a winner. She had always succeeded in anything she put her mind to. Never settling for less than number one, she was at a loss now. She had lost her best friend and now she was about to lose the man she loved dearly.

Talking with Brad yesterday, Icey had found out things that she couldn't believe about Pimp—her so-called husband to be. Brad opened a can of live worms long before the church bombing, but once she got to the funeral and around Jimmy's family did Brad really get to her about Savarous Jones. It was then that Icey was awakened from a vivid dream of pleasure, but it was really pain. Pimp had told her it was heaven but he had shown her hell. He was the perfect mistake that life offered everyone a time or two. He was unbelievable.

She was pregnant by this man. She was in love with this man. She was happy with him. At least that is what she thought, but her thoughts were wrong about what she felt. Everything they had was a lie. Pimp was one big, fat lie from the first day they met.

Why did life have to be this way? Wasn't she this good woman who came up in a close-knit family, well-educated parents and God-fearing? Why did her life, at 28 years old, have to go like this? She was confused as to why. She was stuck on why and it made tears come to her eyes.

She drove until her GPS told her that she was there at the lawyer's office and it was then that she remembered the place before. Icey parked her car. She sat there in the driver's seat, lost in a deep thought. Then, with a silent prayer, she asked God to protect her and forgive her for the act she was about to commit.

She grabbed the Glock nine that sat beside her. She made sure it was ready to shoot; off safety. She slipped it in her purse and got out the car, breathing in fresh air. She was nervous but this was something she had to do. She couldn't let Pimp just continue to be this monster that he was. She just wasn't going for it.

Icey entered the office and was met by the secretary who pointed toward the double doors. She gave a saddened smile and proceeded to the door. When she walked in, Pimp was writing, sitting down. The lawyer was dressed in workout attire. The sweat in result of her workout coated her skin. The lawyer was an older woman but fairly beautiful, Icey noted.

Pimp stood to his feet. He emerged toward her arms open. "Baby," Pimp said.

Tears still fresh in her eyes, Icey fell into his embrace. Being closed in by him made it easy to get her hand on the gun and pull its trigger. This was a crime she just had to commit. She hated that it had to be this way but Pimp left her no other choice.

As bad as she wanted this to be over, said and done, Icey couldn't find it in her heart to do it right now. A sudden fear came over her, making her refrain from grabbing the gun, pulling the trigger. Icey broke down crying. Crying because she was at a loss of everything. Brad was her brother. Pimp was her child's father. She was stuck between a rock and a hard place. She needed God right now because she didn't know what to do. She knew what was right and what was wrong. Pimp was wrong; Brad was right.

"Everything will be okay, baby. I promise." Pimp continued to console her, rocking back and forth as she cried.

Icey hugged him tight, knowing this was the last time she would ever feel this embrace again. "It's so hard right now, Savarous. I can't take it." She cried.

"Let's sit down, baby. Come on." He eased her toward a love seat in the office where they sat. Pimp took her hands into his own as he looked directly at her. "Baby, I love you."

"I love you too, Savarous," replied Icey and squeezed the trigger through her pocket book, striking Pimp in his chest. The loud bang surprised everyone but her. Icey looked at Pimp as he stared at her in pure shock, pure fear, pure confusion.

His body slumped to the floor. He tried to hold on. He tried to fight and be strong, but his body didn't comply.

Pimp

All I can say is *damn!*

How did I not see this shit here coming? All my life I have trained to defeat the opposite side and to take care of myself. One major rule that carried me through life was to never go at it through your emotions.

All I ever wanted was to see my daddy out of this prison shit and free with me. Why was it so hard? Why did people make it impossible? Hadn't my father and I been good men? Lord knows I was scared of this outcome because I knew this life I was living was officially over. I let the woman I love take me out. I mean, she really hit me with one fucking shot. I had no strength. I couldn't put up a fight. I just went out like a bitch. My entire body went numb. I felt nothing but a big let-down. I felt failure at its highest peak.

Icey really shot me? Should have known something was wrong when I saw her with a pocketbook which was something she never carried. I should have known something when I felt her tense up when I hugged her, when her pocketbook was close to me. I didn't think nothing of it though. I was in love with this woman. I didn't think she would cross me, but facts were facts and I knew it was over.

I knew because the first person I saw was my father in his cell doing push-ups. I hovered over him in a mist of haze. The pictures blinked and I saw Yummie. She was looking as good as ever, smiling from ear to ear. She had with her, her best friend who also waved at me, and automatically I waved back. Then, I saw Shaw and every other soul I've ever taken. I saw them and they all greeted me with these warm smiles. This is the one time in my life where I felt cheated, fearful and now more than ever the heart of a gangsta was looking for a God to cry to. I just didn't want my life to end like this.

The End

Submission Guideline.

Submit the first three chapters of your completed manuscript to ldpsubmissions@gmail.com, subject line: Your book's title. The manuscript must be in a .doc file and sent as an attachment. Document should be in Times New Roman, double spaced and in size 12 font. Also, provide your synopsis and full contact information. If sending multiple submissions, they must each be in a separate email.

Have a story but no way to send it electronically? You can still submit to LDP/Ca$h Presents. Send in the first three chapters, written or typed, of your completed manuscript to:

LDP: Submissions Dept
Po Box 870494
Mesquite, Tx 75187

DO NOT send original manuscript. Must be a duplicate.

Provide your synopsis and a cover letter containing your full contact information.

Thanks for considering LDP and Ca$h Presents.

BOW DOWN TO MY GANGSTA

By **Ca$h**

TORN BETWEEN TWO

By **Coffee**

BLOOD STAINS OF A SHOTTA **III**

By **Jamaica**

WHEN THE STREETS CLAP BACK **III**

By **Jibril Williams**

STEADY MOBBIN

By **Marcellus Allen**

BLOOD OF A BOSS **V**

By **Askari**

LOYAL TO THE GAME **IV**

By **T.J. & Jelissa**

CORRUPTED BY A GANGSTA

By **Destiny Skai**

A DOPEBOY'S PRAYER **II**

By **Eddie "Wolf" Lee**

IF LOVING YOU IS WRONG… **III**

LOVE ME EVEN WHEN IT HURTS

By **Jelissa**

DAUGHTERS OF A SAVAGE

By **Chris Green**

BLOODY COMMAS **III**

SKI MASK CARTEL **II**

By **T.J. Edwards**

TRAPHOUSE KING

By **Hood Rich**

BLAST FOR ME **II**

RAISED AS A GOON **V**

By **Ghost**

A DISTINGUISHED THUG STOLE MY HEART **III**

By **Meesha**

ADDICTIED TO THE DRAMA **III**

By **Jamila Mathis**

LIPSTICK KILLAH **II**

By **Mimi**

THE BOSSMAN'S DAUGHTERS **IV**

WHAT BAD BITCHES DO

By **Aryanna**

The Cost of Loyalty **II**

By **Kweli**

A Drug King and His Diamond **II**

By **Nicole Goosby**

<u>Available Now</u>

<u>RESTRAINING ORDER</u> **I & II**

By **CA$H & Coffee**

<u>LOVE KNOWS NO BOUNDARIES</u> **I II & III**

By **Coffee**

<u>RAISED AS A GOON I, II, III & IV</u>

<u>BRED BY THE SLUMS I, II, III</u>

<u>BLAST FOR ME</u>

By **Ghost**

<u>LAY IT DOWN</u> **I & II**

<u>LAST OF A DYING BREED</u>

<u>BLOOD STAINS OF A SHOTTA I & II</u>

By **Jamaica**

Jerry Jackson

LOYAL TO THE GAME
LOYAL TO THE GAME II
LOYAL TO THE GAME III
By **TJ & Jelissa**
BLOODY COMMAS I & II
SKI MASK CARTEL
By **T.J. Edwards**
IF LOVING HIM IS WRONG…I & II
By **Jelissa**
WHEN THE STREETS CLAP BACK
By **Jibril Williams**
A DISTINGUISHED THUG STOLE MY HEART I & II
By **Meesha**
PUSH IT TO THE LIMIT
By **Bre' Hayes**
BLOOD OF A BOSS **I, II, III & IV**
By **Askari**
THE STREETS BLEED MURDER **I, II & III**
THE HEART OF A GANGSTA I & II
By **Jerry Jackson**
CUM FOR ME
CUM FOR ME 2
CUM FOR ME 3
An **LDP Erotica Collaboration**
BRIDE OF A HUSTLA **I & II**
THE FETTI GIRLS **I, II& III**
By **Destiny Skai**
WHEN A GOOD GIRL GOES BAD
By **Adrienne**
A GANGSTER'S REVENGE **I II III & IV**

208

THE BOSS MAN'S DAUGHTERS
THE BOSS MAN'S DAUGHTERS II
THE BOSSMAN'S DAUGHTERS III
A SAVAGE LOVE **I & II**
BAE BELONGS TO ME
A HUSTLER'S DECEIT I, II
By **Aryanna**
A KINGPIN'S AMBITON
A KINGPIN'S AMBITION **II**
I MURDER FOR THE DOUGH
By **Ambitious**
TRUE SAVAGE
TRUE SAVAGE II
TRUE SAVAGE **III**
By **Chris Green**
A DOPEBOY'S PRAYER
By **Eddie "Wolf" Lee**
THE KING CARTEL **I, II & III**
By **Frank Gresham**
THESE NIGGAS AIN'T LOYAL **I, II & III**
By **Nikki Tee**
GANGSTA SHYT **I II &III**
By **CATO**
THE ULTIMATE BETRAYAL
By **Phoenix**
BOSS'N UP **I , II & III**
By **Royal Nicole**
I LOVE YOU TO DEATH
By Destiny J
I RIDE FOR MY HITTA

Jerry Jackson

I STILL RIDE FOR MY HITTA
By **Misty Holt**
LOVE & CHASIN' PAPER
By **Qay Crockett**
TO DIE IN VAIN
By **ASAD**
BROOKLYN HUSTLAZ
By **Boogsy Morina**
BROOKLYN ON LOCK I & II
By **Sonovia**
GANGSTA CITY
By **Teddy Duke**
A DRUG KING AND HIS DIAMOND
A DOPEMAN'S RICHES
By Nicole Goosby

<u>BOOKS BY LDP'S CEO, CA$H</u>

<u>TRUST IN NO MAN</u>
<u>TRUST IN NO MAN 2</u>
<u>TRUST IN NO MAN 3</u>
<u>BONDED BY BLOOD</u>
<u>SHORTY GOT A THUG</u>
<u>THUGS CRY</u>
<u>THUGS CRY 2</u>
<u>THUGS CRY 3</u>
<u>TRUST NO BITCH</u>
<u>TRUST NO BITCH 2</u>
<u>TRUST NO BITCH 3</u>
<u>TIL MY CASKET DROPS</u>
<u>RESTRAINING ORDER</u>
<u>RESTRAINING ORDER 2</u>
<u>IN LOVE WITH A CONVICT</u>

<u>Coming Soon</u>
BONDED BY BLOOD 2
BOW DOWN TO MY GANGSTA

Jerry Jackson